A GU

The main route out of town this way was the old Fort Sanders military road, and Drifter had his horse in a gallop by the time he reached it. Rounding a sharp turn, he saw the phaëton ahead. They were out of town now, and Drifter cut into scrub tinder beside the road, trailing the doctor that way.

He didn't know how far into the first foothills of the Laramies he had followed the clattering rig when the doctor finally stopped there where an old cattle trail crossed the main way. Drifter worked down through the timber until he was near enough to see the faint steam rising from the pair of matched blacks as they stood, champing there in the moonlight. Soon a rider came down the Sanders road from ahead. The tails of his black claw hammer fluttered at his saddle skirts when he wheeled his big roan in toward the phaëton and leaned over to say something. The voice Drifter heard, however, didn't come from there; it came from directly behind him.

"I would deem it a favor, friend,"—the voice was as cold as the click of a cocked gun—"if you would step out into the road, so I can see what I'm shooting at."

LES SAVAGE, JR.

GAMBLER'S ROW

LEISURE BOOKS   NEW YORK CITY

A LEISURE BOOK®

February 2003

Published by special arrangement with Golden West Literary Agency.

Dorchester Publishing Co., Inc.
276 Fifth Avenue
New York, NY 10001

ISBN: 0-8439-5148-6

The name "Leisure Books" and the stylized "L" with design are trademarks of Dorchester Publishing Co., Inc.

Printed in the United States of America.

Visit us on the web at www.dorchesterpub.com.

Table of Contents

/

Gambler's Row

This short novel was completed in late February, 1945. Les Savage, Jr., titled it "Six-Gun Gambler." It was purchased by Fiction House in early March, 1945, and it appeared under the title "Gun-Queen of Gambler's Row" in *Lariat Story Magazine* (7/45). Although this story was written directly following "Valley of Secret Guns," also in this trio, it was published in *Lariat Story Magazine* two months before "Valley of Secret Guns" which didn't appear until the September issue of the same magazine. Its title has been slightly modified for its first publication in book form.

I

The dry heat of a summer breeze blew him into Laramie, and he hitched his bay horse at a rack on Custer Street and went into the Silver Slipper and found the man named Smiles. Smiles took him to the woman's apartment that opened off the balcony overlooking the lower hall of the Slipper. She was sitting on a low Turkish ottoman, and light from the window caught in the abundance of her red hair, done up high on her head.

"Mister Drifter?" she said.

"Miss Warren?" he said.

That seemed to amuse her, and her laugh was as silken as the green velour gown shimmering across her deep bosom. "I admire a discreet man, Mister Drifter, but I think you've seen I am the only one here. If you'll come in, Smiles can shut the door."

The heavy portal made a soft click behind Drifter, and Smiles moved across the room to stand next to the window. This was a typical drawing room of 1870, if a little gaudy, and Smiles made a square, heavy shadow against the dark Indian red of the wall hangings. He shoved a black derby back on his mop of dark hair and twirled a cold stogie between thick lips and pushed aside a bottle-green lapel to hook a blunt thumb in the armhole of his loud checked vest.

"I really expected you a little sooner," said Faye Warren, and the huskiness of her voice only lent it a richness. "When Georgie Kappas came back from Cheyenne, he said you'd be here right away."

"I didn't tell him that," said Drifter. "I only said it sounded interesting and I might look in on it if the wind blew me down this way."

He was becoming more accustomed to the dim light, and he took in the rich cream of her bare shoulders, and that was like a cool drink on a blistering day, and then the pouting curve of her full under lip, and that was like fanning the banked coals of a fire.

She didn't seem to mind his scrutiny. "There were a number of men who didn't have the necessary qualifications for this job. Kappas seemed to think you could succeed where they have failed."

She was appraising him now with cool speculation. He could see her measure the stubborn line to his unshaven jaw, and purse her lips; she watched him read the mature strength in the deep grooves that ran from his long straight nose to his broad, thin-lipped mouth. Then she looked into his eyes, and he could feel her probing to get behind their gray veil, and saw irritation in the slight movement of her hand as she failed.

"You won't be punching any cows." Faye Warren nodded at his dusty bull-hide chaps. "I think the suit should be a dark color. Blue, perhaps. No tails on the coat. Get it at Mannheim's on Cheyenne Street and charge it to my account."

"Aren't we getting ahead of the wagon?" he said.

Her bosom rose perceptibly. "Pardon me."

The acid tone of her voice made him grin faintly, and the caked dust cracked across his leathery face. "A natural mistake. I guess you boss a lot of men here. But before we talk about how you're going to dress me, maybe we'd better see if I want the job."

Smiles took his cigar out and pointed it at Drifter. "We don't talk to Faye Warren like that on Custer Street. Besides owning the Silver Slipper, she happens to be a lady. Maybe you'd better get off your horse and climb on the other side."

"Never mind," said Faye Warren curtly. She sat there a moment, as if deliberately dismissing anger, then she stood, nodding toward the window. "I'll show you."

Drifter's chaps rattled against a rosewood cabinet, following her, and his spike heels sank into the thick Brussels carpet. It brought him close to Smiles, and he realized how the man's singular breadth made him appear shorter than he really was. He almost matched Drifter's six feet and must have topped Drifter by fifty pounds, and his black eyes held a turgid antipathy. The woman pulled back a heavy velvet portière.

"From Fifth Street west to the Union Pacific tracks, Custer Street is known as Gambler's Row," she said, and pointed to where the dusty wheel ruts of Second Street crossed Custer. "The block from Second to First, along Custer, is known as Rot-Gut End, the part of Gambler's Row we above Second would like to forget. At four o'clock on the morning of July Ninth, Gerald Pine was shot and killed at the intersection of Custer and Second. The Row usually closed down about that time, and not many people were on the streets when Pine was murdered. According to reliable sources, it is known that only one man was near enough to identify who killed Pine. This witness has disappeared. Your job is to find him."

Drifter shifted restlessly away from the expensive perfume rising above her coiffure, saw her smile faintly. "It can't be that simple. Wasn't Pine the legislator trying to form a committee to investigate Laramie's board of trustees?"

"Laramie's trustees weren't the only thing Pine's committees were interested in," said Faye Warren. "Laramie's first charter was granted by the Dakota Legislature in December of 'Sixty-Nine, but the lawless element here had already gotten a strangle hold on the town, and the provisional government became so corrupt that after only three weeks the board of trustees and mayor resigned. The charter was revoked, and Laramie was placed under jurisdiction of the federal courts. They put in their own mayor and city commissioners, and have been trying for a year to clean things up without any more success than the municipal authorities had. Last year, when Wyoming was separated from Dakota Territory, Gerald Pine opened his campaign for appointment to the newly created Wyoming Territorial Legislature. The good citizens of Laramie were wild to throw off federal jurisdiction and get another city charter, and would back anyone to the hilt who did it for them. Laramie's one of the largest towns in this section, and its backing was tantamount to election, so Pine began organizing investigating committees, promising to clean up the town and prove to the courts that Laramie was capable of maintaining a charter."

"This lawless element that had gained control. . . ."

"Is centered along Gambler's Row," she said, "naturally."

"Then it was Gambler's Row which Pine's investigations threatened most," said Drifter. "And his death removed the threat? Do you infer that someone on the Row is responsible?"

"It's too obvious for inference," she said. "It's patent that Gambler's Row is mixed up in the murder. That's why we're so interested in getting hold of this witness. You know how inevitable it is that people along a street like this get tied up with one another. What affects one of them affects all. It's that very affiliation which enabled us to control Laramie. But if it's proved that one of us murdered Gerald Pine, or had him murdered, it will be an indictment against all of us. If the Pine faction finds the man who saw Pine's murderer before we do, they have the weapon they can use to wipe us out."

Someone knocked softly on the door. "Judge Pine's outside."

"Gerald Pine's brother," said Faye, looking at Drifter. Then she shrugged bare shoulders. "Let him in."

"He's got his eyes with him."

"You heard me."

Pine came into the room with a hard stride that flapped the tails of his black coat against dusty cavalry boots. For all the authority in his beaked nose and saber-slash mouth, the deep lines of his face held a haggard, driven look, and his eyes burned feverishly from beneath shaggy brows.

"Well, Judge Herman Pine." Faye Warren's voice held a trace of mockery. "It's so rare you honor us with your presence. Drifter, I'd like you to meet the judge. Besides sitting a federal bench, he's an extensive cattle operator."

Herman Pine took an impatient breath. "Never mind, never mind. You know what I'm here for, Miss Warren. I want those I.O.U.s my son, Jim, gave you last week."

Two other men had entered the room behind Pine, looking around the chamber with an habitual care, placing Smiles and Drifter. One of them wore a short black coat with the toe of a holster showing beneath its skirt like the head of a snake poking from a thicket. He moved over beside a richly tufted sofa, plying a toothpick to tobacco-stained teeth.

"The man occupied with his dentifrice is known as Tie-Down Brown," Faye told Drifter sarcastically. "He got the appellation from his talent with a piggin' string. Isn't anybody in Jackson Hole can tie-down a dogie for branding as fast as Brown, they used to say. Only it never seemed to matter whose cattle he displayed his skill on. Maybe that's why he was forced to move down here. Or perhaps it was to be with Edgar Jahare."

Edgar Jahare must have been part Indian. The brim of his black hat flopped down so far it all but hid his glittering eyes, and his face was a swarthy enigma. The nails of his hands that he had hitched into his gun belt were dirty and broken, and he stood with his back up against the wall next to the door.

"You didn't hear me," said Judge Pine.

"I heard you," said Faye. "I'll be glad to give you the chits your boy signed last week. Did you bring the cash?"

"You know I won't have that much cash on hand till after my spring beef are shipped East," said Pine. "I brought my checkbook."

Faye smiled faintly. "The last check you gave me for your son's debts bounced."

Herman Pine's craggy face reddened. "Due to no lack of credit on my part, Miss Warren. You know that. That was

12

just before the courts took over Laramie, and every bank in town was having a run on it. You couldn't have cashed anybody's check here then. You know this. . . ."

"I'm sorry." The hard edge to Faye's voice surprised Drifter. "I've still got that other check of yours, and I can't accept a second. It will have to be cash before the Twenty-Fifth. That's the date on the chits."

"You mean . . . you even got him to date them?"

"No different than a post-dated check." Faye shrugged.

"But you know I can't meet the Twenty-Fifth. . . ."

Drifter sensed a growing calculation beneath Faye's cold smile. "Something similar happened to Judge Paterson here several years back, didn't it? His son or nephew or something got mixed up with a gambling crowd and made so much smell that the judge was dismissed from the federal district and had to take some minor municipal bench. Quite a disgrace. I would hate to sue you, Judge Pine. It would bring to light how much time your Jimmy spends down in the very district you publicly denounce, how many friends he has down here, how much he gambles. That wouldn't set well with the Pine faction, especially at a time like this . . . not very well at all."

Drifter could see the sudden anger turn Pine's feverish eyes dark. Then the little muscles along the ridge of the man's raw-boned jaw bunched up, tightening the skin across his face with a series of palpable jerks. The ball fringe on the sofa twitched with Tie-Down Brown's legs shifting against it. He was watching Smiles intently.

"I should have known . . . I should have known," said Judge Pine in a strangled voice finally. "It's the way you work, isn't it? Do you think you'll compromise me this way? Do you think I'll let a scheming, conniving, gambling slattern like you . . . ?"

"Take it easy," growled Smiles.

Faye Warren had stiffened on the ottoman. "Yes, Judge. You're in no position to take that attitude. You'd better be co-operative. That's what we want from you. Co-operation. You're a key man in the Pine party, and you can do a lot that would benefit us. And you will. A man shall be sent to you in the near future and take you to where you'll get your orders."

"Orders!" Pine's mouth twitched at one corner, and he almost shouted it. "I'll take no orders from you or anybody else."

"I didn't say I would give you any orders," Faye said. "I said you'd be taken to where you'd get them. It's out of my hands now, Pine. I don't even hold the chits any more. I turned them over. . . ."

"To whom?" demanded Pine. "The mythical brains behind Gambler's Row? The boss nobody's ever seen? Don't try to stuff that rot in my duffel bag, Faye Warren. You admit yourselves you've never seen him. He's just a legendary figure concocted by you and Banner and the others so you won't have to take the responsibility for your own atrocious crimes. There's no one behind this but you and your friends. I know you. I know all of you. You murdered my brother, and you thought that would stop what he was doing. It won't. I'll do everything in my power to finish what he started here, and I'll avenge his death if I have to use a gun myself to do it. I thought maybe you'd be reasonable about these chits. I didn't know what was behind it. But I knew you, and I came prepared to do it either way. I'm not going out of here without the chits. If you won't take my check for them, I'll. . . ."

Faye's laugh was as cold and hard as the diamonds on her fingers. "You can't be serious. A federal judge doesn't resort to violence. Think how it would affect your position if it were revealed that you entered a lady's premises and intimidated her. Worse than having it known your son frequented Custer Street."

The mockery of her voice had drained all the blood from Pine's face, and he was trembling violently. Edgar Jahare took a breath that pushed his belly against his heavy gun belt, and he was watching Drifter. The ball fringe dangled back and forth as Tie-Down Brown took a step away from the sofa, then stopped dangling.

"You're right," said Pine gustily. "A federal judge just doesn't resort to violence. That's why no one will believe your claims of intimidation. My brother Gerald's mistake was doing this thing honorably, Miss Warren. I've tried to do it the same way, but I'm through now. I'm playing the game your way, and I'll get the same results you do. Any suit you bring will have to go through the municipal courts, and they're my friends on the bench, not yours. Accept my check for those chits, and I'll not cause you any trouble. Otherwise, I've got more men outside, and I'm ready to get what I'm after any way you want me to."

Tie-Down Brown and Edgar Jahare had placed themselves with a tacit understanding from the beginning—Jahare against the wall by the door, facing Drifter, Tie-Down farther on by the couch with the room clear between him and Smiles. But a man drawing against the wall would strike his elbow, and Jahare was obviously too experienced to make that blunder, and Drifter saw where Jahare would be if he took one step away, and knew their mistake lay in that.

"Smiles," said Faye coldly. "Show the gentlemen out."

Tie-Down stopped picking his teeth. Drifter took a single easy step that placed him beside the shimmering French gray of a wing chair's damask arm.

The judge waved a gaunt hand. "I warn you, Smiles. Don't move. We came for those I.O.U.s, and we aren't going till you hand them over. I warn you. . . ." Smiles took the first step, and Pine's head jerked up. "All right, Tie-Down."

Tie-Down was facing Smiles when he went for his gun, and Jahare took that one jumping step away from the wall toward Drifter and drove for his own weapon. It put Jahare in front of Tie-Down, and, when Drifter bent and heaved the chair up off the floor and spun it into Jahare, the Indian went backward into Tie-Down with a shout, his gun going off at the ceiling. Tie-Down staggered back into the sofa with his six-shooter pinned between his own body and Jahare's, and the sofa tipped over beneath Tie-Down's weight, and both men tripped over it as they went backward, and fell, and the chair crashed in on top of everything else.

Even before the chair had struck Jahare, Drifter had leaped toward Judge Pine, catching his coat by the collar. He pulled it down with a jerk, turning the sleeves inside-out down to Pine's elbows and pinning his arms there. It had all been done in the time that it took Smiles to get his gun from beneath his bottle green coat, and he stood there with the wicked little Bulldog revolver in his square hand, looking very foolish without anything to shoot at.

Faye had stiffened on the ottoman, without time to rise, and suddenly she burst out laughing. Pine's face turned purple. He still had his hand on the gun he was going to draw, but couldn't lift his elbow high enough to pull it on out, and he jerked spasmodically from side to side, cursing bitterly. Drifter twisted his fist in the collar, holding it down beneath the man's shoulder blades, rendering the judge's struggles futile.

"Anything else you want with this man?" he asked.

Faye was laughing so hard she could hardly answer. "No, no. He'll come around, but I think we're through for today. Take him out, Drifter, take him out."

Drifter jerked Pine around, calling to Jahare. "Never mind, Edgar."

Jahare had just gotten from beneath the chair and was pawing for his gun. He stopped a moment to look at Drifter. Then he got up carefully, leaving the weapon on the floor. The fall had taken the edge from Tie-Down's enthusiasm, too, and he stood up, breathing heavily.

"Damn you, Drifter, I'll have you hung for this. . . ."

"Shut up, Pine," said Drifter. "Get going."

Jahare's boots made a soft sound against the Brussels carpets, backing out. Tie-Down's heavy-shouldered silhouette blocked the door a moment. Drifter followed them with the helpless judge, going clear down the balcony to the head of the stairs with him that way.

"You got more men downstairs?" said Drifter. "You tell them to get out before I let you go."

Judge Pine struggled for a moment, then turned to Tie-Down, saying bitterly: "All right. Go on down and tell Knox to get his men out."

Tie-Down moved down the stairs and through the thin afternoon crowds in the Slipper's lower hall, and Drifter could see him speak to a man here and there, and soon a little bunch gathered at the front door, and pushed through. Drifter let go of Pine and turned his back on whatever it was the judge said and returned down the balcony. The door closed on the faint sounds from below. Smiles still stood at the window with a frustrated look on his face.

"You can put your gun away now, Smiles," chuckled Faye. "Take a lesson from Drifter. It would have been very indiscreet to shoot a federal judge, no matter how he came in here." The smile she turned on Drifter was warm and personal. "Kappas said you had the necessary qualifications for the job. He was right, Drifter, he was most certainly right."

II

Peter Poker was playing solitaire at a deal table near the foot of the stairway, a dapper little man with red gaiters holding up the sleeves of his striped silk shirt. He took care of the Slipper's poker lay-outs, and his supple hands were famous from Montana to Mexico.

" 'Morning, Drifter. It looks like they finally got you into civilized clothes."

Drifter's broad-shouldered, lean-hipped frame looked well in the dark blue suit he had gotten at Mannheim's, but he still felt uncomfortable, tugging self-consciously at a black string tie. " 'Morning, Peter. How're the aces?"

Poker did something with the deck of cards and turned up an ace of spades. "Slick as bear grease. I hear you really started out with a bang, yesterday. I hear Smiles is going to take lessons from you on handling irate court judges and their bad hats without using a gun."

"Come on," Smiles told Drifter thinly, as he moved past the poker lay-outs through the big empty hall with its four glittering chandeliers. Drifter was about to follow when Poker crooked a slender finger at him, speaking softly.

"You want to watch the smiling boy there. He is extremely disgruntled at your showing him up in front of Faye yesterday, and I am free to admit that of all the men in this world who have some small skill with a shooting iron, it is Smiles who I would least like to have disgruntled at me. I would liken him to a snake, only he never rattles before striking. If he were the kind to cut notches on his gun for every man he has liquidated, he would have whittled away the butt long ago. You want to watch him."

"Thanks for the tip," said Drifter, "only I don't see why it should come from you. I just got on this wagon, and you and

Smiles have been riding it a long time."

In lay-outs like this, there was usually an undercurrent of professional jealousy among the housemen, and, in the glance Peter Poker sent after Smiles, Drifter saw it. Perhaps Peter coveted Smiles's position with Faye.

"All right, Peter." Drifter laughed softly, and went on across the room, pulling his new white Stetson down against the hot blast of noon sun as he pushed through the batwings and out onto Custer, catching up with Smiles and moving down through the sounds of an awakening Row. The batwings on the Poker Pot across the street popped dismally as a swamper shoved through them, latching them open to the outside walls. Wyoming dust roiled up in ashen eddies from beneath the creaking wheels of a big Murphy wagon piled high with yellow hay. Drifter glanced at the bag Smiles carried.

"We bank messengers this morning?"

"Never mind," said Smiles, and turned across the corrugated ruts of the street to Orin Banner's Poker Pot.

The saloon echoed hollowly to the men's boots. Smiles told Drifter to wait at the bar and headed for the potted palms at the rear that must have screened the office door behind them. A bald-headed barkeep in a dirty white dinner coat was setting out pretzels and cold meat. Drifter looked at the loquacious Irish curl to the man's mouth and decided he would talk without much prodding.

"Orin Banner has a nice place here," Drifter said, leaning his elbows on the bar. "He's the big boss of Gambler's Row?"

The barkeep spun an amber glass of beer across to him. "Big boss? Why?"

"It looked like Smiles was paying off."

The barkeep shrugged. "They all do. Ten percent every

month. That don't mean Banner is top cheese. He just handles the money."

"For whom?"

"You're Faye Warren's new man?" said the barkeep. "Drifter? My handle's Jigger. Got it from tossing them across this bar, I guess."

"I imagine," said Drifter. "Faye Warren sit the big horse?"

"No," said Jigger. "Not Faye Warren or Orin Banner or Kings Nixon."

"You don't want to name him?"

"I couldn't," said the barman.

"Who could?"

"Nobody," said Jigger. "Nobody knows who bosses Gambler's Row."

"Isn't it rather naïve of you folks to hand over ten percent of your take each month to someone you never saw?"

The barkeep shrugged. "We get results, don't we? Nobody bothers Gambler's Row. Not the municipal authorities or the territorial tall hats or the federal badges. Gerald Pine got ideas and look what happened to him. We do just about as we please. That alone would be worth ten percent of any man's poker pot. Where else would you find a town in which the gambling interests don't tip their derbies to the city authorities? But it don't stop there. We get protection from each other. In any other burg you'll find the saloons cutting each other's throats worse'n Comanches loose with Bowie knives. Any place else, I'd be charging you a nickel for that beer, trying to undercut the dime the Silver Slipper would charge. Here it's twenty-five cents everywhere. You can see how that benefits the operators. It's just an example."

"But if Orin Banner handles the monthly donation from the operators, it seems he'd know who he turned it over to."

" 'Morning, Jack." Jigger nodded to a man in a pin-striped

frock suit who had walked by them, holding a black bag similar to the one Smiles had carried. "Happy Jack brings in the ten percent from Lazy Ike's. No, Drifter, Orin Banner doesn't know any more than the rest of us. Two men come for the money. Nobody in town knows them or where they come from or where they go. Some have tried to find out where they go. Never came back to tell. Most of us here just let it alone. What good would it do us to know who handles things? Whoever it is, they do a good enough job. It wouldn't surprise me if Gambler's Row has control over all of Wyoming Territory before we're through. . . ."

Jigger stopped talking, but his mouth stayed open. He was looking over Drifter's shoulder. Drifter turned around, and Smiles was standing there, antipathy in his black eyes.

"You talk too much, Jigger," he told the barman. Then he shifted his gaze to Drifter, and he shifted his stogie to the other corner of his mouth. "What's your hand in this, Drifter? You seem mighty interested in things."

"Faye told me to go with you this morning and find out the things I needed to know and meet the people I needed to meet," said Drifter softly.

"No," said Smiles. "No. Something more. I never saw a man take such an interest in this job before. You got a boot of your own stuffed in the poke? Why did you come down here in the first place?"

"For a hundred a week and keep," said Drifter.

"Is that all?" said Smiles, and reached up to put the tip of his thick index finger against Drifter's chest. "There are a lot of people you don't need to meet, and a lot of things you don't need to know, and, if I was you, I wouldn't ask too many questions."

Drifter reached up and curled his hand around Smiles's finger, pushing it away from his chest. "That's a bad habit to have, Smiles. It might irritate somebody sometime."

Smiles winced and tried to pull his finger out of Drifter's big hand. It wouldn't come. He jerked back violently. Drifter let go the finger. It took Smiles off balance, and he stumbled back two or three steps before he could stop himself, and even before he stopped, his hand was going for his coat. Then that stopped, too, and he stood there with the tips of his fingers beneath the bottle-green lapel.

"Go ahead," said Drifter.

His elbow had shoved the tail of his own coat off the butt of his Rogers and Spencer, and his hand hung near enough to the big .44. Orin Banner had come from his office behind the potted palms, and he made a big, rigid figure back there, dissipation drawing insidious lines in his florid face. Jigger had his hands flat on the mahogany bar, and his Irish mouth was open.

"Go ahead," said Drifter.

Smiles looked at Drifter's eyes. A gunsmoke color had turned them cloudy. Smiles looked at Drifter's hand. Then Smiles took his own hand out, drawing a slow breath. There was no fear in his voice when he spoke.

"Someday," he said heavily, "I will."

Kings Nixon's Full House was just west of Second on Custer, in the beginnings of Rot-Gut End. Planks covered the glass of one window where it had been broken, and the slats of the batwing doors had all been knocked out, and the reek of whisky and stale tobacco struck Drifter with a physical force as he stepped inside. There were no roulette lay-outs or faro tables, only a few poker games. One man stood at the sagging bar, picking his teeth.

"Well, Tie-Down," said Drifter. "You working a double shift?"

Tie-Down Brown removed his toothpick to spit. "I'm a freelance, Drifter. Judge Pine just wanted that one bronc' peeled yesterday."

"You didn't peel it," said Drifter.

"There's more ropes on the fence," said Tie-Down. "Maybe I'll take another throw soon. Kings's beer better than the Silver Slipper's."

"Where is Kings?" asked Smiles.

Brown's boots made a sloppy sound against the rotting floor, moving in front of the two men, and he ignored Smiles, speaking to Drifter. "Kings doesn't want to see anybody today. You better untie your dally from around this one, Drifter, before it gets snubbed so close nobody'll be able to unwind you. Everybody on Gambler's Row knows why you're here. There's a lot more to this than just finding that missing witness to Gerald Pine's murder. Ask the three jaspers who had a whack at the job before you. Or maybe you hadn't better. They couldn't tell you anyway. They couldn't tell anybody. You don't want to be put in that position, do you?"

"Orin Banner said Kings didn't ante his ten percent yet," said Drifter. "We came to get it."

"I'll do the talking," said Smiles, stepping forward.

"No," said Tie-Down. "I will. You aren't getting anything."

"Let's go back to the office," said Drifter.

"I'll do the talking," said Smiles.

"No," said Tie-Down. "Let's not."

"Let's go back to the office," said Drifter.

Tie-Down had opened his mouth to say something. He must have seen Drifter's eyes. He looked at them a moment. Then he closed his mouth, shrugging, and turned toward the sagging door at the rear of the bar. Smiles turned to Drifter before they followed the big man, his words hissing out between his teeth.

"Will you keep your damn' yap shut? I told you, I'm handling this."

"All right," said Drifter. "You handle it."

Smiles hesitated, patently not knowing how to take that, then he went after Tie-Down with short, stiff paces. Kings Nixon was a picture of refined dissolution, tall and slim in striped morning pants and black frock coat, sitting with his patent leather boots propped on a big battered Chippendale desk, languidly cleaning his fingernails. His black hair was shot with gray at the temples, and his long nose seemed to have been provided for the sole purpose of looking down it. Smiles went up to the desk and put both his square hands flat on the scarred surface.

"Orin Banner said. . . ."

"That I didn't ante up this month," said Kings disinterestedly. "I don't mean to."

"Others have tried playing solitaire," said Smiles. "Sammy Willow did. . . ."

"And Sammy Willow doesn't any more," said Kings, taking particular pains with a pink thumbnail. "And Sammy Willow's Big Jug doesn't any more. I know, I know. I'm not Sammy Willow. I'm tired dumping ten percent of my monthly pittance into a pot I can't even see. I've had enough of taking orders from Faye Warren and Orin Banner. Just because they're the biggest operators on the Row doesn't mean they have any more right to hand out the chips than I do. The only one giving the orders is the brains. From now on, the only directions I consider will be the ones I get direct from him. Now, if you'll be kind enough to leave. . . ."

Smiles took one of his hands off the desk and shoved back

a lapel to tuck his thumb in the armhole of his vest. "Not without the money."

"Don't make a mistake, Smiles," said Nixon.

"This ain't your Silver Slipper," said Tie-Down.

"No," said Kings. "This isn't your Silver Slipper. Maybe you can rake in Judge Pine's chips there. Not mine here. I've got three stout barmen out there with shillelaghs that have laid many a better man than yourself beneath my poker tables." He raised his voice slightly. "Mike."

Tie-Down had closed the door behind them when they came in, and had moved to one side of the room where Drifter had to turn away from the door to see him. Now, when the portal opened behind him, Drifter didn't have to look to know that the man standing there was Mike, and that there were two others with him, and that, if he turned to get them in sight, it would put Tie-Down behind him. He could see the tension stiffen Smiles's thick shoulders, and knew it would be a mistake to let this get much further out of hand.

Either way Drifter turned now, he would have men at his back, and he didn't think they would let him do any turning anyway, from now on. He had spotted the half-empty bottle of port on the desk by then. He was glad it wasn't whisky. The whisky bottles were too short. The long-necked bottles were ideally suited.

"What's given you such big ideas all of a sudden, Kings," said Smiles.

Nixon reached a bored hand inside his pocket, removed a signet ring, tossed it indifferently on the desk. "Faye and Banner will leave me alone from now on. Just give that to Faye. She'll know what it means."

Smiles looked at the ring, put it in his pocket. "Faye will get it. Along with the money. Whatever this means will have to wait. The men are due to hit Banner's any day now for the ante. If it's not a full pot, there'll be more hell to pay than Gambler's Row ever saw on ten Saturday nights. I'm giving you a bigger break than I should, Kings. I'm giving you another chance to hand over the money."

"This isn't your Silver Slipper, Smiles," said Tie-Down.

"No," said Nixon. "This isn't your Silver Slipper, Smiles."

"No chairs to toss around now, Drifter," said Tie-Down.

Tie-Down's presence there drew Smiles around to see if Drifter had Tie-Down, and that was Smiles's mistake. Tie-Down laughed shortly. When Smiles saw how Drifter was caught, he must have realized he had let it go too far, and then must have realized how he was caught.

"Don't turn around, Smiles," said Nixon. "I'll let you get out now. I'm through talking, and you can go if you want to. Don't turn back around."

"No," said Smiles in a hoarse voice, and whirled, and tried to dive sideways out of the line of fire and draw all at once. He got his bulldog revolver out past his lapel. Then Nixon had whirled and knocked the gun up by the simple expedient of lifting his feet off the desk, and the bulldog went off at the ceiling. Drifter's voice came before the gunshot was dead.

"All right. I can have this in your face before your boys drop me. Better tell them to put it away, Nixon."

If Drifter had turned either way to draw his gun, he would have been taken from behind. Perhaps it was that his move had been so unexpected, or so fast. It had taken them enough by surprise to give Drifter that extra second, and he had reached the desk before either Brown or Mike could make their move. At the same time Smiles had drawn, Drifter had jumped to the Chippendale and grabbed the wine bottle and cracked it on the edge of the desk, and now he held the bottle's long neck fisted, and its smashed end still dripped red port into Kings Nixon's lap.

"Yeah," gasped Kings. "Yeah, put it away, Tie-Down, my God, put it away."

There was nothing in the world like broken glass in a man's face to bring his fear out. Sweat beaded Kings's pale brow, and he sank his chin into his neck, trying to lean back from the jagged end of the bottle. Drifter heard the sibilant squeak of a gun sliding into its holster behind him.

"Come around where I can see you," he said.

Tie-Down moved down the side wall, breathing in a heavy, frustrated way, still holding onto the butt of the gun he hadn't freed in time. Mike was a bucolic specimen in a dirty apron and faded blue shirt, as tall as Nixon, but gangling where Kings was slim and stooped where Kings was straight. He and the other two housemen held wicked-looking shillelaghs in their hands, leaning forward tensely, glancing from Nixon to Drifter. Trembling with rage, Smiles bent to pick his gun off the floor.

"Now," said Drifter, and jammed the bottle closer to Nixon's face. "How about the money?"

III

Faye Warren sat on the blue satin sofa, looking at the buckskin bag Drifter had brought from the Full House, laughing softly. "Not many men would have done that to Kings, Drifter. He's drunk most of the time and he's got delusions of grandeur and he runs the rottenest penny-ante dive on the Row, but not many men could do that to him."

"Tie-Down Brown was at the Full House," said Drifter. "Would that imply a connection with Judge Pine somewhere?"

"Oh . . ."—Faye waved a white hand—"we've always suspected Kings Nixon of stooging for the Pine faction, but the fact that Tie-Down was at Nixon's doesn't prove anything. He hires out to anybody who'll buy him beer, and, when he isn't working, you can usually find him at the Full House."

"Whoever runs your show seems to take care of things smoothly," said Drifter. "I shouldn't think he would let Tie-Down get away with riding in Pine's string yesterday."

Faye's voice suddenly lost its warmth. "Nobody gets away with anything. Tie-Down will be taken care of."

"By whom?"

The woman spoke up sharply. "Smiles told me you seemed interested. How should I know? Nobody knows. Banner and I just get our orders and pass them on to the rest of the Row. You'd better pull in your horns, Drifter. It isn't a healthy curiosity."

Drifter shrugged. "There was something else. How about the ring, Smiles?"

Smiles moved stiffly across the room, fished the ring from his inside pocket. Drifter couldn't read the expression that crossed the woman's face; the sofa creaked beneath her stiffening body. Then she nodded her red head sharply at the buckskin bag, and her voice was strained.

"Take it back. Right now. Take it back to Kings."

"That's why he got such a swelled head all of a sudden," said Smiles.

"What is it?" asked Drifter.

"Nothing," said Faye. "Just take the money back. You heard me."

"Faye," said Drifter. "You aren't dealing me a straight hand in this. If I'm going to find your missing witness, I want to know all you can tell me. I'm working blind enough as it is. Tie-Down said three men died on the job before me. You didn't tell me about them."

Anger darkened her blue eyes till they were almost black. "I didn't think it would matter."

"It wouldn't," he said. "That isn't the point. How can I work for you if you're going to hold out on me? You must see what a position that puts me in. Did you hold out on those other three? Is that why they got dusted? I can't work for you and buck you at the same time. How about the ring? Does it belong to the man you're hunting?"

She inhaled sharply. "Man? We haven't narrowed it down that far. We know only one man saw the shooting, but we don't know which man he is. A hundred men must have left Laramie that night. We've traced most of them. It was a job that only an organization such as we have here could have done. We've eliminated all but three who can't be accounted for. Albert Afton. Professional killer, gambler, rakehell. He was as permanent a resident here as you could find in an itinerant town, and his complete disappearance should have some significance. Edward Lederer. Penny-ante cattle operator who hasn't yet returned to his home spread above Cheyenne. He was last seen at the cattle pens on the night of the shooting, about four hours before it happened. Dean Remington. Worked in the Hackett Livery on Grant Street. . . ." She looked up suddenly. "Mean anything to you?"

"Should it?"

"You had such an odd look on your face. Do you know Remington?"

He shrugged, trying to keep his voice indifferent. "It's not an uncommon name. Which one of these three does the ring belong to?"

She paused before answering. "I didn't say it belonged to any of them." She rose stiffly, and the green velour of her long

29

gown made a restless sibilance across the carpet to the window. She stood there a moment, one hand on the velvet portière, looking out. Then she took a heavy breath. "All right. All right. This Dean Remington. Just a kid. Twenty, maybe. Used to come to the Slipper. Got sort of a crush on me, I guess. Never gambled or drank or anything. Just showed up on the lower floor at eight o'clock every night, seven nights a week, waiting for me to come down. I tried to get rid of him gently, but he was in a bad state. Then, the night of Pine's murder, the boy tried to give me the signet ring. My initials are on it, you see, in gold. Diamonds. Everything. No telling how long he'd saved to get it. Hackett doesn't exactly pay his stable hands a fortune. I told the boy I couldn't accept it. He took it away with him before I had a. . . ."

She stopped, and for a long time neither of them spoke, then Drifter ran the tip of his tongue across dry lips. "And he's one of the men you can't account for. The fact that Kings Nixon has this ring would imply that Nixon knew where the boy was, and that the boy is the missing witness?"

"Oh, you and your implications!" She turned on him furiously. "This doesn't necessarily imply anything. The boy could have lost the ring, and Nixon could have found it."

"Not *any* implications," he said. "Yours. This whole thing is built on them. *If* there is a witness, and that witness can identify someone on the Row as the murderer of Gerald Pine, and the Pine party gets hold of that witness, they'll use it as a weapon to wipe out the Row. *If* Nixon's possession of the ring means he knows where Dean Remington is, and *if* Remington is the missing witness, then Nixon is dynamite."

"Of course, of course," she said. "From the beginning, it's all been implications, supposition, ifs. That's why we couldn't afford to take a chance. We didn't know anything for sure. We had to follow every possible lead. That's why we can't afford to take a chance now. If Nixon knows where the witness is, and we make a wrong move against him, it would be slitting our own throats. All he has to do is tell the Pine party where the witness is and the Row is finished. But it doesn't have to mean Remington is the one. The whole thing could be a bluff. Nixon's bluffed before. Just because Nixon has that ring doesn't mean he knows where the boy is, and just because he's using it this way doesn't mean Remington is the witness. But we still have to handle Nixon as if that were so, and he knows it, and that's why you're taking the money back."

"Edward Lederer always seemed the more logical witness to me," said Smiles sullenly. "He left without taking the cattle he'd contracted for, his horse was in Hackett's, and his belongings still in his room. Remington, on the other hand, paid up his rent and took his duffel and his horse like any ordinary man leaving town would."

"Why would this witness disappear?" asked Drifter.

"Either he knew how dangerous it would be to stay, or someone got hold of him," said Faye.

"Someone like Nixon?" asked Drifter. "If Nixon's keeping him staked out somewhere, he'd have to keep in contact. Who works for Nixon?"

"Nixon wouldn't trust anyone," said Faye. "He wouldn't even trust his own barmen. They're too stupid for anything as lethal as this. Nixon always does his own business himself."

"Nixon made any trips lately?"

"Hasn't left Rot-Gut End in the last three years," said Smiles contemptuously. "I don't think he's even been out of the Full House in that time."

"At least you haven't seen him go out."

"We've kept check on him," said Faye. "He's caused

trouble like this before, and Orin Banner got orders to have a man watch Nixon. Nixon never varied his habits. Up at twelve and sitting back there in his office drinking rot-gut until four in the morning. Mike closes up then and goes home, and Nixon goes to his room on the second floor of the Full House and smokes a cigar for fifteen minutes and turns out the light and goes to bed. We've got it all down on paper. That's how we keep the reports when a man's watched. Banner's agent watched for three weeks from the Cosmopolitan Hotel across from the Full House."

"Where does Mike live?"

"Nixon's barkeep? In the Brady rooming house across the U.P. tracks. We had him tagged, too. You're up against the fence, Drifter, and it hasn't got any gate. Turn your horse around and take that money back to Nixon. And I'd advise you to quit worrying about this. Nixon isn't your job. You know what your job is."

Drifter was looking at her with narrow eyes. "I'm not so sure I do, now."

Down past Rot-Gut End, a cattle train hooted mournfully in the chill morning darkness. A last drunk stumbled out of the Full House and wandered aimlessly up Custer toward the better end of Gambler's Row. Mike backed out of Nixon's place, tall and awkward in the gloom, letting the slatted doors slam behind him and latching them. He shut the outside door and locked it. His feet made a hollow clatter down the plank walk toward the tracks.

"I thought you'd be doing something like this," said Faye Warren.

Drifter whirled toward her, slapping at his gun in some automatic reaction. Then he relaxed, crouching there across the street from the Full House in the alleyway between the Cosmopolitan Hotel and Lazy Ike's Saloon. The woman must have come up behind him, and in the dark he could barely make out the tight buckskin riding pants she wore, with a square-cut ducking jacket of blue denim over her flannel shirt. She pointed up to the second story of the Full House where two lighted windows made their yellow rectangles. The tall figure of a man was silhouetted for a moment in one, then moved on.

"Nixon can't contact anybody up there. Don't you think you'd better come back and get your sleep now?"

Drifter lifted the buckskin bag that Nixon had put his ten percent in the day before. "I have to pay him back first, remember? You wait here?"

She started to answer, but he was already out of the shadows and moving across Custer. There was another alley behind the Full House, and a rickety stairway leading up outside the building to the second-story porch there. The steps popped rottenly beneath Drifter's boots going up. He hadn't yet reached the top before the light dimmed out. He was beyond the door when it opened.

"All right," he said. "Drop your own and move back in."

The man who had opened the door had taken a step out with a snub-nosed Derringer in his hand, and he stood rigidly there for a moment with Drifter's gun pressed into his back. The Derringer clattered against the porch floor. Drifter followed him in and told him to light the lamp.

"Well," he grinned. "Came to pay Kings back his money. Does he do this every night?"

Mike stood there with his mouth hanging open stupidly, glaring at the big Rogers and Spencer .44 in Drifter's fist. It would take a stupid man, thought Drifter, to have come out on the porch that way.

"I guess I won't leave the money, Mike," said Drifter.

"You just stay here a while unless you want your dinner pushed out backwards."

He picked up the Derringer, going out, and got down the stairs and ran towards the Cosmopolitan. Faye met him in the middle of the street.

"Ever notice how much Mike looks like Nixon?" asked Drifter. "Put Kings in Mike's coat and stoop him over a little and you couldn't tell the difference on a dark night."

"Mike?" she said. "Why? What's happened?"

"That's Mike in Nixon's room," said Drifter, and he was moving down the street toward the only horses in sight, a trio of dusty cow ponies hitched in front of Lazy Ike's Saloon.

"What are you doing?" panted Faye. "They hang horse thieves."

"We haven't time to round up our own animals," he said. "I can't do any tracking till daylight, and that's two hours off. I'll have to see Nixon if I'm going to tail him anywhere."

"You speak as if you're going alone," she said.

Mrs. Brady's rooming house was on Cedar Street in the shanty district between the tracks of the Union Pacific and those of the Laramie North Park and Central. Nearing the two-story structure, Drifter reached and caught the bridle on Faye's horse, hauling it down to a padding walk.

"If that was Nixon who came out of the Full House," she said, "what makes you so sure he went down here?"

"For three years, Kings Nixon and Mike have never varied their routines," said Drifter. "You told me that. It's become a standing joke along the Row. And now Nixon is using that. It was so well-established that you would have been satisfied to go home when you saw Mike's shadow in Nixon's window. That's what Nixon wants. The whole idea was to throw off any watcher by appearing to follow the identical routine they both have had for so long. I'll give you odds Nixon takes the same trail Mike has been taking, till he gets to Mike's rooming house, at least. Any animals in this district?"

Her face was a pale enigma in the darkness. "All the houses in this district usually have a horse or two shedded out back."

He turned up First and entered the alley that ran behind the houses fronting on Cedar; they dismounted and led their horses cautiously down the dark lane, filled with the nauseating odors steaming up from open piles of garbage and manure.

Drifter pointed to the rear of the Brady rooming house ahead, whispering: "That back stairway's covered, and it opens right into the shed. If it's where they keep the horses, a man could go to the shed from his room and have the animal saddled without anybody spotting him. . . ."

He broke off suddenly, grabbing her horse by the bridle again and hauling it behind a fence two houses from the Brady place. Standing there, it came to them again, the muffled stamp of a horse from somewhere ahead. Then a door creaked mournfully. Drifter heard the woman's sharply indrawn breath as a shadow separated itself from the huddled blackness of the fences and sheds ahead. For just that instant, the dim form of a mounted man showed in the alley, then it was gone. The whole thing happened so quickly and had such a ghostly quality that Drifter couldn't have sworn he saw it.

"Where did he go?" whispered Faye.

"Tighten the nosebag on your nag and hold him down," Drifter told her, notching up a strap on his own mount, a chunky little pinto with a long black mane. Then he swung on and necked it out into the alley. They came up with the shed behind the Brady house; directly across from it was a lane leading between two railroad shops of the Laramie North Park and Central. Moving through the blackness, Faye's horse reared suddenly. She brought it down, reaching forward for the headstall. From somewhere ahead came the whinny of another horse. Drifter was holding his pinto's head down and could feel its neck swell with trying to answer, but the tightened noseband prevented that. They waited there a long time before the soft thud of hoof beats from ahead broke the silence.

"Stopped to listen," said Drifter. "He didn't hear anything."

They halted at the mouth of the alley while the rider ahead made his dim shadow trotting across the gleaming rails and past the roundhouse, disappearing finally into the cottonwoods standing in the creek bottoms westward from the railroad yards. Drifter waited as long as he dared, then quartered toward the roundhouse itself so as to put it between them and the trees. They trotted around the far side, the horses shying to the sudden hiss of steam from a freight engine inside. They went at a walk through the cottonwoods to Custer Creek. Drifter splashed through and went down the opposite bank till he found water gleaming across a stretch of shale where the rider had come out. They took the slope to the crest of the slope beyond. Standing in the shadows of poplars here, they could survey the expanse of the Laramie Plains stretching west. Drifter nodded to where the rider made a small blot crossing the gray blanket of short grass between them and the Medicine Bows.

They would make their own sign against the downward slope, so Drifter found a coulée and followed its bottom into the flats, then rose to level ground and trailed the other through the morning darkness without much chance of being spotted.

"You seem to be acquainted with this sort of thing," she said.

"I've done my share of trailing," said Drifter.

"And traveling." She smiled. "That saddle you sit so well looks like Texas."

"The best double-barreled roper Porter ever made," he said. "They wouldn't have a center-fire rig south of the Red River. Lucky to have found one on this borrowed horse."

"You don't often see a Rogers and Spencer around these parts, either," she said.

His hand slid across the walnut grips of his .44. "I got that from a man in Kansas. He had some notches carved on the handle, but I figured I couldn't lay claim to them, so I put on some new grips."

"You *are* a drifter." Her voice was strangely husky. "And when this job is done, the wind will blow you onto a new pasture. You're tough enough when you want to be, and it looks like you've had experience in handling most things that come up in a place like the Row, but somehow I get the impression that you don't belong with a crowd like that, Drifter. Your hands look more to me like dally ropes and stamping irons than cards and chips. It seemed to me you'd come from more . . . honest jobs."

He looked at her sharply. "That sounds funny from you. Do you consider yourself dishonest?"

She hesitated a moment, then laughed. "I'd never thought of it much one way or the other. I suppose the bad ones just naturally gravitate to Custer Street. Maybe the fact that a person works there makes him dishonest."

"Not necessarily," he said. "I don't think dishonesty is that easy to define, or honesty. I think it has a lot to do with what you believe in. I think you're that way, Faye. I think you do things according to your own lights and don't bother much whether anybody else thinks it's right or wrong, bad or good. Which is more honest, the gambler who drinks his liquor in public or the parson who locks the door of his room before he takes his little nip?"

"Ah," she said, "a philosopher."

The mockery in her voice stiffened him for a moment. Then he relaxed, grinning. "What's the matter, Faye? Afraid to talk with a man about anything except business?"

He saw her fist tighten on the reins. "Afraid? Don't be naïve."

She rode on in a strained silence, and he knew he had touched her, and it gave him a sense of triumph, because he had the impression, somehow, that not many men could touch her.

Dawn was silhouetting the pine-crested line of the Medicine Bows by the time they reached the foot slopes. The man was out of sight in the timber above, and the last they had seen him he had been lining straight for the hogback. Drifter avoided the open parks, climbing through the aspens on the lower slopes and then into darker juniper thick with alligator bark and finally into sighing lanes of lodgepole pine. They dismounted below the crest and climbed to the ridge afoot, bellying down there so as not to be skylighted. The rising breeze swept across the valley below and ahead, flapping the brim of Drifter's white Stetson. Then, on the ridge opposite, a rider skylighted himself for a moment, and was gone. The woman started to move. Drifter caught her arm.

"That's an old come-on," he said. "A trailer seeing a skylight like that would rush to follow as soon as it was gone, and, if the man over there had stopped his horse on the other side and crawled back up to the ridge, he could see the trailer lining down this slope plain as day. You told me Kings was smarter than he looked."

"That makes two of you." She smiled. "But if he didn't stop, we'll lose him."

"Not ridge-topping like this," he told her. "It takes a man beneath a long time to get out of sight of the top lands. We stay above, and we have the advantage."

They lay there another ten minutes, then Drifter pointed to the shadowy flutter of birds settling back into the timber on the opposite hogback. They dropped into the valley and rode up to that next ridge, and took three more that way, seeing the man skylight himself beyond each time, and lost him on the fourth. They crouched a long time on that last top, waiting for the quarry to appear beyond. Finally Drifter nodded to the thick green of cottonwoods in the valley.

"He's under them, going up or down. Let's take down first."

They followed the ridge down several miles, keeping on the near side so as not to show themselves, but found no sign. They turned back, passing the place where they had halted, going on until they saw that the ridge they rode was a spur, melting into the main range that ran at a right angle from them. The valley below rose to become a low saddle through the mountains ahead; beyond the saddle, the Medicine Bows rose in a pristine tumble of snow-capped summits and black-timbered slopes. They had risen above the saddle before they saw the cabin tucked into the coulée down below.

They tied their horses to a pine, and Drifter got the saddle-gun from the black-maned pinto he had taken, and began working down through the timber. He didn't try to stop Faye from coming, because he knew her willfulness by now, and how useless argument would be. They reached timber edge and looked across a park of blue root juicy enough to make a heifer drool. Drifter worked around by the empty pack pole corral and came into the house from its blind rear, Winchester cocked.

There was something waiting about the mordant silence. Drifter stopped by the bark-chinked wall of peeled juniper logs, listening. No sound. He moved around the front, rooting a rock from the ground, kicking it across the open door. There was no reaction from that, and he moved inside. Two bunks stood at the back wall and a three-legged stool had been overturned by the iron wood stove. A faded denim poke lay by the plank table, some belongings spilled out of its open mouth; a pair of boots lay beneath the table. Faye came in, and he turned to her with a wry grin.

"Looks like somebody left in a hurry. Whoever it was, we must have missed them by a horse hair."

His eyes were accustomed enough to the gloom to see the delicate flush of anger tint her cheeks, and she kicked at the poke on the floor, thick red hair bobbing against her shoulders with the violence of her movement.

"Damn," she hissed, and kicked at the war sack more viciously, "damn, damn, damn. . . ."

He began to chuckle. "You're all woman, aren't you, Faye?"

She looked at him sharply, lips pouting. "What do you mean?"

"Cold as the ice in Jigger's Scotch one minute," he said, and moved closer. "Hot as a juniper the next. I thought I'd known all the icebergs till I saw you that first day. Then you switched ends like a sunfishing bronc' and turned on a smile that would melt the Missouri in January, and I thought I'd seen everything. I'm glad I stayed around to see you mad. You've got more woman in you than any ten I've ever known all put together, Faye. It would take something of a man to tame you, wouldn't it?"

She took a step backward, bosom rising beneath the flannel shirt. "Are you making love to me, Drifter?"

The mockery was in her voice again, and he flushed, realizing how far he had let himself be carried away. "When I make love to you, Faye," he said softly, "you won't have to ask me whether I am or not."

"You. . . ."

That's all she got out. He had his hand over her mouth, carrying her up against the wall. She struggled in his grip; then he saw her eyes widen above the top of his hand. It came for the second time, faintly, the nicker of a horse. Drifter shoved the carbine into her hands, putting his lips close to her ear.

"You're staying here this time. I'll call before I come back. Anybody tries to come in without calling, you know what to do with this saddle-gun."

He turned and took a step out the door, meaning to slide along the wall, because the horse had called from somewhere behind the shack. But the man was across the clearing, standing up from the boulders, and Drifter hadn't yet begun to pull his gun free in that first step, and that was how they saw each other.

"Drifter," said the man, and hauled for his iron.

The echo of Drifter's Rogers and Spencer cracked back and forth between the rock faces rising on either side of the saddle, and the man had fallen over on his face before they ceased. Faye had caught up with Drifter by the time he reached the man.

"I'll have to tell Smiles how quickly you can get your gun out," she said dryly. "He hasn't seen you do it yet."

Drifter looked at her sharply, wondering what it was that had suddenly rubbed his hair the wrong way. She was looking at the man on the ground without much expression on her

41

face. Drifter hunkered down and turned the man over. Dirt smudged his face, and blood, but even in death Drifter recognized him.

"Know him?" he asked the woman.

Her voice sounded strained. "Albert Afton."

"That simplifies things," said Drifter.

"How do you mean?"

"Afton was one of the three men you thought might be the witness," he said. "This leaves two in our duffel bag."

"Where did you know him before?" she asked.

Drifter was looking at her again, still trying to find what it was he disliked here. "Know him?"

"He knew you," she said. "Why did he pull on you like that, Drifter?"

He understood what it was now. The sight of death seemed to have absolutely no effect on her. The realization of that filled him with a heavy, nameless oppression, and he stood up, shoving his gun away.

"I have an idea most men who knew you wouldn't pull a gun on you like that without a good reason," she said.

"Maybe he didn't expect to see me."

"No." She shook her head, a cold speculation entering her eyes. "I have an idea it would take more than mere surprise to make a man who knew you pull on you. What was it, Drifter? What's your hand in this?"

IV

Gambler's Row hit its stride about ten o'clock that night, and Orin Banner's Poker Pot was packed batwings to walls. Sweating muleskinners shoved their red-shirted shoulders through milling cowpokes who raked the floor with dangling spurs. Pot-bellied townsmen added the pungent reek of cigar smoke to the stench of plugs and cigarettes and whisky and perspiration.

"Fifteen on the black," called a croupier from his roulette lay-out somewhere in the mob. "The black has it, and the number is fifteen."

Drifter bellied up against the smooth mahogany and hooked a heel into the tarnished brass rail, calling for beer. While he was drinking, a pair of cowpokes came up beside him. The tall one ordered two fingers of rye without a chaser.

"Find your horse, Carver?" Jigger asked him, spinning him the rye.

Carver tossed off the drink, grimaced. "Yeah. Found them this afternoon staked out in that bunch grass south of town. All I remember is hitching them in front of Lazy Ike's last night about eleven. We didn't sober up till this morning around six, and they were gone then."

"What kind of nag you fork?" asked Drifter.

"Pinto with a black mane," said Carver. "Looked like he'd been ridden some to death. I'd like to get my hands on the dirty hoss thief that did it."

He moved away into the crowd with the short 'puncher, and Drifter grinned wryly at himself in the mirror before he downed the beer.

Jigger passed by, cleaning glasses with a swift skill. "Are you working for Orin or Faye?" he wondered. "You spend more time over here than you do at the Silver Slipper."

"You serve the best beer on the Row, Jigger," said Drifter. "How about another?"

Jigger slapped the bung-starter, looking at Drifter closely. "You ain't letting your curiosity run away with you?"

"As to what?"

"Like I told you, Drifter, other jaspers have tried to tail

those two gents who come after the money every month. I never saw said jaspers in here otherwise. I'd hate to be losing as good a customer as you."

Drifter was looking past Jigger into the mirror. The man reflected in the glass was moving through the crowd behind Drifter, tall and suave in a black claw hammer and black flat-topped hat, a small, clipped mustache accentuating the sardonic curl of his lip. Drifter quartered through the crowd to meet him.

"Kappas," he said. The man didn't seem to hear him, and Drifter moved directly in front of him, catching his arm. "Georgie. When did you trail in?"

The tall man raised a dark eyebrow. "Afraid you have the wrong party, friend."

"What?" said Drifter. "Kappas. . . ."

The man had shaken off his arm and was swallowed by the crowd. Drifter looked after him, rubbing his jaw. He went back to the bar and got his beer.

"Do I look drunk, Jigger?"

Jigger was mixing a Scotch and soda. "This is only your second beer."

The tall man with the black claw hammer had disengaged himself from the crowd now, and pushed open the door to Banner's office, barely discernible behind the pattern of potted palms. Drifter slid down the bar a way. Another man was moving toward the palms. Drifter tabbed the scar down one cheek to remember later, and then the pair of ivory-handled Colts strapped higher on his waist than most professionals usually carried their work. He went behind the palms, too. Drifter put his beer down and moved away from the bar.

"Drifter?" said Jigger.

The stairs on the right-hand side led to a balcony over the bar from which the door of the men's room opened.

Coughing in the foul tobacco smoke, Drifter went to the wash
rack near the window, shoving open the sash as if to get fresh
air. The door kept banging open as men came in or left, and
the incessant buzz of talk rose and fell over the dry shuffle of
feet. Drifter took his time washing his hands, and he kept his
eyes deliberately turned to the window until they were accustomed to the darkness outside. There was an alley running
between the Full House and Sammy Willow's empty Big Jug
next door; four windows from Banner's place cast their
yellow squares of light across the blackness down there.

Drifter was drying his hands when the creak of an opening
door below came to him. He leaned on the window frame,
rolling a cigarette. The man coming from the side door of
Orin Banner's office made a soft thud stepping into the alley.
He passed through the square of light from the first window,
leaning to one side as if to compensate for a weight he carried.
He passed through the second square, and Drifter caught the
claw hammer tails on his black coat. Something made a
clatter at the end of the alley that opened into Kearney. The
man passed through the final light. The squeak of buggy
springs came to Drifter, then the clatter again. When the man
again passed through the light of the first window nearest
Kearney Street, he wasn't leaning sideways. The door below
creaked once more, and the buzz of talk rose about Drifter
again, and the dry shuffle of feet.

Drifter reached the barroom in time to see the man in the
claw hammer come out of Banner's office and move casually
toward the front doors. In a moment, the man with the high-
slung Colts came out.

Drifter waited behind the batwings until he saw them get
their mounts from the hitch rack and turn east on Custer.
Across the street, the flickering oil lamps lining the gaudy
façade of the Silver Slipper threw their garish light across

Drifter's own bay horse hitched among the other animals there. He backed the animal out and turned to follow the two men through the crowds churning Custer's ashen dust.

Gambler's Row ended at Custer and Fifth, and at Sixth one of the men ahead halted his horse, while the second continued on. The one who had stopped turned around in his saddle. The crowds had petered out up here, and Drifter was the only mounted man on this block. He kept his horse going ahead at a walk, passing the other. It was the one with the Colts strapped high. As Drifter crossed Sixth, a two-horse phaëton turned out of Kearney Street and came the single block down Sixth and turned into Custer, springs squeaking.

" 'Evening, Doc."

The doctor nodded absently to Drifter, muttering— *"Bon soir."*—and clattered on by at a smart clip, a neat little Frenchman in his trim gray frock suit and his white goatee. Drifter watched the phaëton reach the second rider ahead, and heard another greeting. He didn't want to lose sight of them, yet he realized he was not in the best position, with that man wearing the Colts behind him. He turned into Ninth toward Fort Sanders and pulled up at a hitch rack. He waited there some minutes, but the second man didn't pass. When he went out into Kearney again, none of them was in sight.

The main route out of town this way was the old Fort Sanders military road, and Drifter had his horse in a gallop by the time he reached it. Rounding a sharp turn, he saw the phaëton ahead. They were out of town now, and Drifter cut into scrub timber beside the road, trailing the doctor that way.

He didn't know how far into the first foothills of the Laramies he had followed the clattering rig when the doctor finally stopped there where an old cattle trail crossed the main way. Drifter worked down through the timber until he

46

was near enough to see the faint steam rising from the pair of matched blacks as they stood, champing there in the moonlight. Soon a rider came down the Sanders road from ahead. The tails of his black claw hammer fluttered at his saddle skirts when he wheeled his big roan in toward the phaëton and leaned over to say something. The voice Drifter heard, however, didn't come from there; it came from directly behind him.

"I would deem it a favor, friend,"—the voice was as cold as the click of a cocked gun—"if you would step out into the road, so I can see what I'm shooting at."

It must have been the house of some big cattle spread. It was tucked away in the secretive timber of a deep valley, guarded by the jealous spires of the Laramie Mountains. There were a lot of shadowy horses stamping at the hitch racks along the stone porch, and guards appeared from the trees. There had been other guards at the entrance to the valley, and Drifter understood how impossible it would be for anybody to get in here, even if he could find it. George Kappas rode on one side of Drifter, tall and sardonic in his black claw hammer and flat-topped Stetson. He had gotten a black bag from the doctor's phaëton and slung it on his horse.

The man with the Colts strapped high had been the one who had come up behind Drifter. "I thought you looked interested there in Custer Street," he had said, when Drifter moved out onto the road. "I pulled into an alley when you turned into Ninth, and, when you came out again and went after the phaëton, I trailed you. We kill 'im, Kappas?"

"No, Meades," Kappas had said. "We had better take him along."

Drifter had tried to speak with Kappas several times, but the man remained silent. Now, pulling up to the porch, they dismounted. Drifter didn't get to see the face of the guard at the front door. The living room was twice as long as it was wide, with a huge stone fireplace at one end, the light from the crackling blaze playing fitfully across the restless crowd of men in the room. A big white-haired man in old-fashioned cavalry boots threatened to collapse an ebony reception chair near a closed doorway; several more spread their pompous posteriors against the chintz sofa. The pegged boards squeaked beneath the nervous tread of a man pacing up and down with his hands clasped behind him. Drifter felt their eyes on him as he was led to a brass-bound door. There was a guard before this portal, too, a Winchester hooked in one elbow. He opened the door to Kappas's nod.

The second room was smaller, with a large Oriental screen done in black and gold cutting off one whole side. Kappas went behind the screen, carrying the black bag, and Drifter heard him talking to someone in a low voice. He came out in a moment, indicating that Drifter should take the chair by a shuttered window. Sitting down, Drifter felt the sweat break out on his palms. The whole thing was turned eerie by the re-strained silence. Kappas opened the door to the living room and beckoned someone in, saying nothing.

The man's mutton-chop whiskers twitched nervously as he came through the door, and he stiffened perceptibly as the portal made its velvety click, shutting behind him. With the same impersonal nod of his sardonic black head, Georgie Kappas indicated the newcomer should be seated in the wing chair before the screen. The voice from behind the screen startled Drifter. It was husky and muffled, and oddly familiar.

"Mayor Fitch? I'm glad to see you've come. But then you always do, don't you? I understand there's some trouble."

The little man in the wing chair pulled at his whiskers. "Yes, yes. Trouble. Always trouble. You know the city engineers were down inspecting the buildings along Custer last week. They condemned Banner's Poker Pot and the Cosmopolitan Hotel. If they put that in their report to the federal courts, you'll have an injunction issued to tear the buildings down."

"Did they commit an estimate of what it would cost to rebuild the Poker Pot and the Cosmo in order to meet federal specifications?" asked the voice from behind the screen.

"Yes, yes. Approximately twelve thousand for Banner's place. Twenty for the hotel."

"And how much would it cost to see that the engineer's report to the courts didn't include the condemnation of those buildings?"

"But they're fire hazards," said Fitch. "You know what happened when the old Comanche Inn burned. A hundred people. . . ."

"Never mind. I know you aren't worried about that. How much?"

Fitch cleared his throat, eyes shifting to Kappas, then back to the screen. "Haldane's chief engineer. I've already felt him out. He mentioned five thousand."

"I thought you had," said the voice. "That would be cheaper than rebuilding the condemned places. He said five thousand? He'll take twenty-five hundred if he sees it in cold cash."

"That's not the real trouble," said Mayor Fitch. "The courts are sending government auditors down to make their semi-annual check on our books next week. The city treasurer's been doing a lot of juggling for you. . . ."

"You mean for *you*." The voice had an edge that drew a look of pain to the mayor's face. "We know how heavily you've drawn on the municipal coffers for your personal debts, Fitch."

Fitch held up a plump hand. "No, no. . . ."

"Yes, yes. Never mind. We can't afford to have the courts find your books out of balance. After all, if they can't trust the man they appointed mayor, who can they trust? How much will it take to straighten up your books?"

Fitch took a relieved breath. "There are several contracts I've put off. One to Carry for that sewage disposal on Custer. . . ."

"How much?"

Fitch cleared his throat. "Ah, about twenty-five thousand. . . ."

"I'll give you fifteen." The voice was flat, cold.

Fitch half rose in his chair. "But that won't. . . ."

"You can cover your deficit with that. We know how much you've spent personally since the last meeting, Fitch. You were extended credit in Laramie and your bills ran around twenty thousand. With the five thousand you got from us last time, that would leave fifteen thousand you appropriated from municipal funds. It's all you'll get. Anything else?"

Fitch settled back, taking a heavy breath. "One more item. . . ."

"You mean your pay? We'll consider the fifteen thousand your cut this time."

Fitch jumped to his feet, waving his hands. "But . . . but. . . ."

"That's all," snapped the voice. "Only don't think you can get it this way by fiddling with the city's books again. Another mistake like that and the courts will be looking for a new man to run their city. I'm giving you the bag with the chief engineer's twenty-five hundred, and the fifteen thousand you'll need. There's a pen and paper on the table. Make out the usual receipt."

★ ★ ★ ★ ★

After Mayor Fitch had left, Kappas motioned in another, the big white-headed man who was, it seemed, the chairman of the Laramie Cattleman's Association. He was given money to stifle a report to the government inspectors of Texas fever cropping up in herds owned by a corporation affiliated with the gamblers on the Row. And after the cattleman, came the city comptroller, and after him, the sheriff of Albany County. As they came in, one by one, getting their money and their orders, and leaving, the whole amazing pattern was unfolded for Drifter, the incredible machine that had been built up until it held all of Albany County in its grip. It wasn't the board of trustees that ruled Laramie, or the county commissioners, or even the federal courts. It was whoever sat behind that screen. The muffled, unrecognizable voice held all the cold, passionless intelligence it must have taken to build such a brilliant, complicated mechanism and keep it running so smoothly. Each man to come in, big or small, strong or weak, was instantly rendered subservient by the menacing command of that voice. Then Kappas ushered the last man into the room.

Judge Herman Pine stopped just inside the door, the haggard, driven lines etched more deeply into his gaunt face, his black tail coat hanging slack from a stooped, weary frame.

"Drifter," he said dully. "I might have known."

The voice from behind the screen turned Pine. "Sit down, Judge. You've made a wise decision."

Pine's boots had a harried sound against the hooked rug, moving to the chair. "Decision? It was no decision. You know that. Faye Warren said I had to contact you. You have those chits my boy signed?"

"And they are yours for a little co-operation, as Miss Warren undoubtedly told you."

51

Pine dropped into the chair, leaning forward with his head in his hands. "You've got me over a barrel, damn you. I tried to fight it. I wasn't going to come with the man you sent for me. I was going to turn him over to the marshal. But already it's begun to start. Just the rumor that my son's been seen on Custer, and my friends are already beginning to avoid me on the street. A justice from the appellate court was down yesterday to drop the hint that they couldn't have a man on the bench in this district who had any connections with Gambler's Row. If those chits are made public, it would be my ruin."

"I'm glad you understand all the ramifications," said the voice. "But you'll have no worries, if you play along. We have four chits signed by your son. Let's say you will render a service for each one. Tonight you'll get the first. Before he died, your brother Gerald had petitioned the federal district court to issue an injunction prohibiting the sale of liquor in Laramie after twelve midnight. Ostensibly the act was for the morale of the soldiers at Fort Sanders who had been getting into trouble on the Row, but really it was only another of Gerald Pine's attempts at cleaning out the Row. He knew that half the take of the houses along Custer comes after twelve, and that it would be a mortal blow to the gamblers if they couldn't sell drinks after that time. You will see that the petition gets sidetracked."

Pine drew a thin breath, and Drifter could see the struggle that was going on inside the man. Pine ran his fingers through thick gray hair, shaking his head. Finally he straightened.

"All right," he said. "All right. That petition is in my court now. I'll take care of it."

"Fine. Here is the first chit."

Kappas went around behind the screen and came back with a piece of white paper. Pine looked at it for a moment, then turned sharply and rose, opening the door himself. Through the opening for that moment, Drifter could see that the outer room was empty. Pine was the last one, then, and the others had left as they had gotten their orders. Drifter felt his lank frame growing rigid in the chair. Him, now?

Kappas closed the door, went behind the screen. There was the low buzz of voices. Drifter licked dry lips. He brushed a damp palm across the lip of his empty holster. Kappas had his Rogers and Spencer. Then the door burst open and Meades shoved in, both ivory-handled Colts in his hands, shouting: "There's a bunch of horsebackers fogging in by the river road and more up past the corrals. That Judge Pine must have had them trail us in when we brought him. They're all around."

A shot sounded muffled from outside, another. There was a scuffle behind the screen, and whoever was back there spoke sharply. "Pine?"

"He's away," said Meades. "I sent Oswego with him down the road."

Whatever the person behind the screen would have said was cut off by a thunderous volley of gunfire from out front. A guard with a Winchester staggered backward through the front door, firing, and fell full-length on his back. The rush of men across the front porch made a heavy clatter. Their guns filled the living room with a deafening roar. The oil lamp on the table by Drifter was blasted to tinkling shards, and the darkness that fell in the room was complete as Meades slammed the door. Slugs made their dull tattoo on the oak panels. Meades grunted sickly.

Drifter had jumped toward the screen when somebody called—"The window!"—and a heavy body careened off him, running toward the window, knocking him aside. He tripped and fell across someone stretched on the floor. Meades?

Then the screen was toppled over on him, and someone else ran by. He realized that they had come from behind the screen, and that was who he had come to see in the first place, and he didn't intend to lose him now. He pawed around for one of Meades's Colts and whirled after the shadowy figure. The first to go out the window was Kappas, tearing off the bar on the shutters and slamming them open, silhouetted in the moonlit square for that moment as he crashed bodily through the glass, claw hammer catching on the jagged edges. His gun began going as soon as he hit the ground outside.

Then the second silhouette, slim and lithe, twisted around for a moment jumping through, and was gone. That was the one who had come from behind the screen, the one who ruled Laramie, the one Drifter wanted.

Drifter went headfirst out into the rocking gunfire and hoarse shouts and pounding beat of running horses, rolling when he hit the ground and coming up with the figure he was following still in sight. A pair of riders quartered in from around the house, their guns stabbing redly at him. Drifter zigzagged and took a snap shot at the tail man and saw him go down and then was past them. The two running figures ahead were heading for timber. The first one disappeared into the pines, and Drifter didn't care about him. It was the second one he wanted.

A man came running across from the corral above the house, shouting something. He stopped and got down on one knee, and the moonlight glinted on a carbine as he took aim at the running shadow ahead of Drifter. Drifter turned, still going forward, and emptied Meades's gun at the man. He didn't know which shot caught him. When he dropped the Colt, he saw that the man was down on his belly with the carbine beneath him. Then Drifter sprinted on after that figure ahead. They had reached the first trees when he caught up, diving for the running legs.

They rolled into the blanket of pine needles and came up against a shaggy trunk with a force that brought a sharp gasp from the one beneath Drifter. He stopped rolling with one arm caught beneath the person's hips, and he suddenly realized how soft they were. Then he saw the face twisted toward him, a pale blot in the gloom, taking him a moment to recognize it.

"Faye!" he gasped.

V

The window was open and, from outside, came the faint, early morning sounds of Custer Street. Batwings creaked on Orin Banner's Poker Pot as a swamper pushed out and slopped a pail of dirty water into the gutter. A heavy wagon creaked past. Faye Warren sat on the Turkish ottoman in her apartment, still dressed in leather leggings and denim ducking jacket. She waved her third cigarette at Drifter where he stood at the window.

"You see now why I couldn't tell you a lot of things about this job."

"You're the brains behind the whole set-up," Drifter said, and shook his head, grinning wryly. "It's fitting, in a way. It would take a feminine mind to evolve such an intricate machine. It's even bigger than most people suspect, isn't it? You must have strings on every official in Albany County. Handling all those men, though, wouldn't someone recognize your voice, sooner or later?"

"Did you?" she said. "No. Kappas rigged me up with an old carney horn stuffed with muslin. It would muffle anyone's voice beyond recognition. Kappas and Meades were the only men in the world who knew I was the brains behind the Row."

She glanced at Georgie Kappas, where he sat on the arm of the gray wing chair. He had been the other man running into timber with Faye the night before and had gotten horses from where they must have had them staked in the trees. Drifter had mounted tandem with Kappas, and Faye had taken the other animal, and, working into the timber upslope, they had managed to escape Pine's men.

"Smiles . . . ?"

"Knows nothing," said Faye. "He's my man here at the Slipper, that's all. Kappas and Meades weren't known here. That gave them a freedom of movement which any man known in Laramie wouldn't have. That's why I kept them in Cheyenne most of the time, where Kappas told you about the job. That's why Kappas wouldn't recognize you in the Poker Pot the other night. He and Meades had come for the money. I have to put up ten percent just like everybody else to keep everything looking right. Having Banner hold it like that makes for even less chance of someone else suspecting me."

"The doctor?"

"Doctor Lafarge is in with the gamblers along the Row, but we only use him up to a certain point," said Faye. "He's only a blind to carry that money out of town. Nobody looks for a doctor to be doing that. Kappas takes the bag out that alley beside the Poker Pot to the doctor's rig on Kearney Street, then Lafarge takes it to the crossroads where Meades caught you last night. That's as far as the doctor goes. That's all he knows. The guards at the house last night are the same way. They're Kappas's men, from Cheyenne. They never get inside the second room. They don't even know what they're guarding. Kappas pays them well, and they don't ask questions. Even if they did drop word of where they'd been, it wouldn't matter, because we meet at a different place every month. That house belonged to the chairman of the cattleman's association you saw."

"The kind of trick Pine pulled isn't done often," said Kappas thinly. "And you saw how much good it did him. He did put on a good act, though, didn't he? I thought he was a beaten man."

"He's not a beaten man," said Drifter. "He's a driven man. And you'll drive him too far one of these days, Faye. Did you see his eyes? Looks like he's got some sort of fever."

She shrugged. "It's too bad he did that last night. I really don't want to ruin him. Get a new judge on the bench in this district and we'll have to start all over again."

"I understand the other men who got curious about what happened to that money haven't been seen around since," said Drifter. "You eliminated them?"

"Not personally." The woman's voice was cold. "I couldn't afford to have them come back, though none of them ever got as far as you, Drifter." Someone knocked on the door, and Faye turned to Kappas. "Get out the back way. I don't want Smiles or Peter seeing you. I'll contact you in Cheyenne as soon as I need you."

The rich, buttoned pattern of Indian red wall covering so cleverly hid the door set in the back wall that Drifter hadn't known it was there. Kappas pressed on one of the buttons, and the portal clicked open, revealing a narrow stairway. When the door had closed behind the man, Faye ground out her cigarette on a silver tray.

"Yes?"

Smiles's voice came from outside the front door. "Kings Nixon is downstairs."

"Bring him in," said the woman, and turned to Drifter.

"You do the honors. I don't want him to see me in this outfit."

She went into her boudoir, closing the door, and in a few moments Smiles came with the owner of the Full House. Kings Nixon walked into the room jauntily, the picture of refined dissolution, tapping the end of his gold-headed cane against the knife-edge crease of his trousers.

"I understood Faye was in."

"She'll see you in a minute," said Drifter, and saw Nixon's gaze caress the whisky decanter on the low marquetry table. "Have one?"

"My father taught me never to drink before breakfast," laughed Kings. "But I never eat breakfast anyway. You might pour one about . . ."—he measured it with a thumb and forefinger—"that big."

The Pinch bottle made a dull clink against the ivory inlay on the table. Nixon took the drink and sat down on the edge of the ottoman, carefully pulling up his trouser legs to preserve the crease. He held the whisky up to the light from the window, smacking his lips in a genteel way. Suddenly he stood up, bowing.

"Ah, Miss Warren. . . ."

"Never mind, Nixon," said Faye, coming in from her boudoir. "You weren't in the other night."

Nixon smiled enigmatically, turning slightly to Drifter. "No, I wasn't. I understand Mike didn't make as gracious a host as he might have. I'll see that he mends his manners."

Faye had changed to a house gown of blue cashmere and had done her red hair up in a high chignon, and Drifter found it hard to believe she hadn't slept all night. She sat down at the other end of the ottoman, offering Nixon a cigarette, taking one herself. He lit it for her with a flourish.

"You came after the money?" she said.

"You understand," said Nixon. "Is that what Drifter had come with the other night?"

"What's your game, Kings?"

Kings raised his brows. "I don't have a very big house, Faye, you know that. Poker, mostly. . . ."

Faye waved her white hand irritably. "You know I'm not talking about that. We've beaten around the bush long enough."

Holding his cigarette between two slender fingers, Nixon put his right hand on top of his left across the gold head of the cane, and leaned forward on it. "They gave you the ring?"

"Why else should I send your money back?"

Nixon smiled. "Then you must know what I'm playing, Faye."

"You think we'll meet your demands because you know where the witness to Gerald Pine's murder is?" she asked. "How can we know you know? How can you prove Dean Remington is the one?"

"That's for you to worry about, my dear," he said softly. "I don't have to prove anything. I don't have to do anything. I don't have to say anything. It's all right there on the table. If the Pine faction found the witness, you and everybody else on the Row would be through."

"Rot-Gut End is part of the Row."

"Slitting my own throat?" Nixon smiled. "You couldn't exactly say I have much to lose. A lot, however, to gain. I've been wanting to move up this way a long time. A higher class establishment, you know, one more fitting to my abilities. Chandeliers, dancing girls, roulette."

Faye's lips made a thin line. "You're playing with a bunch of three spots, Kings. You can't take any hand with them. You meant your possession of the ring to imply that Dean Remington is the missing witness? He's only one of three we

59

couldn't trace. How about Edward Lederer? Albert Afton?"

"Yes, how about Afton?" Nixon's short laugh might have meant anything. He put his cigarette to his mouth for a deliberate draw, then lowered his hand to the cane once more. "You know what my possession of the ring implied, Faye, and all you're doing here is arguing with yourself. You know you can't afford to offend me. . . ."

"We work 'im over?" said Smiles, raising a languid finger to the faint scar crossing his narrow cheek.

"If you recall, Smiles," Nixon said, "several mysterious gentlemen tried to do that without much success, more than once in the past. I have an idea, somehow, that the so-called brains of our illustrious little organization must have sent them. It would be more dangerous than ever to try that now, wouldn't it? For if I did happen to know who this witness is, or where he is, I could have arranged it so he would be turned over to the Pine faction the moment there was any threat made to my person, couldn't I?"

Faye dismissed that with a wave of her hand. "We know, Nixon, we know."

"I think you do," said Nixon, and put his smoke carelessly in the ashtray. "Aside from the money, now, when do you think I could move into the old Big Jug next to Banner's place? It's rather a boorish name, and I'd change it, of course, but the house is large enough, and it's been empty since Sammy Willow disappeared last January. I like the location."

"Nixon!" Faye leaned forward sharply. Drifter could see the rise of her bosom. Then she took a careful breath. "All right. All right. You'll have to talk with Banner about the Big Jug. He controls the lease. Tell him I sent you."

"And the money?"

"Smiles will get that for you."

Nixon rose, bowing. "Fine, my dear, fine. I'm glad you are

taking such a co-operative attitude. You must drop into my new place sometime. I assure you the bottled goods will be of a higher quality than the Full House has been offering."

The restraint Faye kept on herself was palpable in the rigid line of her body and the white band of flesh around her lips as Smiles ushered Kings out and shut the door behind them. The woman let a hissing breath out between her teeth, jerking from side to side in a frustrated way, grinding her half-smoked cigarette viciously into the ashtray. She rose and moved in front of Drifter to stand at the window, breathing heavily. They could see Kings come out of the front door below and cross Custer toward Orin Banner's Poker Pot farther down. On the opposite curb, Nixon stopped to tap at his pants cuff as if brushing off some dust, then he turned and moved jauntily down the walk, swinging his stick.

"As if he owned the Row already," said Faye thinly.

She was near enough to bother Drifter with her perfume, and his voice sounded thick. "You going to let him get away with it?"

"No." Faye turned to him. "I'm not. As Kings said, several others have worked him over from time to time in the past. One of them even died in the attempt. Kings is more dangerous than he appears. But you're dangerous, too. I think you can do a lot of things for me where other men have failed. I want you to get rid of Nixon."

He couldn't help stiffening, and he knew she saw it. That speculation darkened her blue eyes, but she waited for him to speak. The violent anger had left her now, and once more she was cold, calculating, passionless.

"If Kings came at me with an iron and there wasn't any other way out, I'd pull on him," said Drifter. "I've done it that way before more than once, when I was working for somebody else, or when I wasn't working for anybody. But

61

you can't hire me to go out and burn a man down in cold blood."

Faye's teeth made a milky shadow against the red of her rich under lip, biting it. "You're still working for me?"

"I usually finish what I start."

"I imagine." Her voice was cold and hard as six-gun iron. "This is how it is, then. I can't afford to have anyone on the outside knowing that I run the Row. You understand that. Now that you know who I am, if you're working for me, you're working for me the whole way, and you'll carry out any order I give you. If you aren't working for me. . . ."

Her coldness raised an anger in him somehow, and he reached out and caught her shoulders, feeling their warmth through the gown. "If I'm not working for you, what? You wouldn't let me leave Laramie alive, is that it? I've been wondering what you'd planned for me last night, if Pine hadn't broken it up. And if I am working for you, what? Will you hold out on me like you've been doing? I can't fight you as well as everybody else, if I'm going to work for you, Faye. You've got to be square with me. You know Remington's the man you want now, don't you?"

Her face, turned up to him, flushed hotly. "There's Lederer. Let me go!"

"No," he said. "From the minute Nixon sent that ring to you, you knew it was Remington who saw Pine murdered. Not Afton or Lederer. Remington! Why else would Nixon have this hold over you? If you know it's Remington, Faye, tell me. . . ."

She was struggling in his grip, pain mingling with the anger flashing through her eyes. "Drifter, let me go. What's Remington to you? Why should it affect you like this? Let me go. I don't know it's Remington any more than you do. It might as well be Lederer. We can't afford to take a chance, that's all. If it is Remington, and we moved against Nixon and didn't make that move final, Nixon could finish the whole Row by letting Pine know of Remington's whereabouts. That's why we have to make our move final. You'll get rid of Nixon. You're the only man who can do it. Let me go, damn you, let me go. . . ."

"No!" he shouted hoarsely, swept with a rage as violent as hers. "You're lying to me. I want to know, Faye. It's Remington, isn't it? I'll find out, Faye. I'll find out if I have to tear your whole town apart with my bare hands."

Her body was up against his, writhing in his grasp, and he didn't know how it happened exactly. Maybe it was that the desire to do it had been held in him for so long now, and that rage was one form of passion anyway. Whatever it was must have swept her the same way. She had suddenly quit struggling, and her face was turning up to his, and for that moment she gave him all the richness he had known was there.

Then she tore her mouth away from his, and freed herself so viciously that she crashed back against the window frame. She stood there, palms flat against the wall, her whole body shaking with the terrible intensity of some violent emotion. When she spoke, her voice came in a bitter gasp.

"Get out. No man can do that to me, Drifter. Get out!"

In the hall below, Peter Poker leaned disconsolately on his lay-out, sipping a beer and waiting for the dribble of afternoon players to begin. Drifter closed the door of Faye's chamber behind him, leaning heavily against it for a moment, breathing hard. Why did it have to be she? He shook his head angrily, and walked toward the head of the stairs. He had drifted so long now, taking their kisses and leaving them behind with no more regret than he left the dust of the road. And now, Faye. . . .

He was halfway down the balcony before he became aware of Smiles. The man had been standing at the head of the stairs, and he had been staring intently at Drifter with a strange, taut expression on his face, and suddenly he began to walk toward Drifter. It struck Drifter then that, from where he had been standing, Smiles could have seen into Faye's room as Drifter came out, could have seen Faye still standing with her back to the window that way.

"Did you get ideas?" asked Smiles.

They met, facing each other midway between door and stairs, and Drifter tried to read the man's heavy face. "About what?"

"About Faye," said Smiles. "I've been wanting to talk with you about her, Drifter. You don't want to get ideas about her."

"Whatever ideas I have about Faye are my own," said Drifter. "Or maybe you have ideas."

Smiles put his forefinger against Drifter's chest. "I know my place, Drifter. I'm just a funny man with a derby and a cigar, and the only thing I ever made a success at in life was what Faye hired me for, and you know what that is. The only time Faye ever thinks about me is when she needs me to do it, and by God I will do it if you don't leave her alone."

Drifter wrapped his hand around Smiles's finger and shoved it away from his chest, using it to push Smiles backward. "That's a bad little habit of yours. It's liable to irritate somebody, someday."

"And I told you I'd pull on you for that someday!" shouted Smiles, tearing his finger free and jumping on back, "and I'm doing it. . . ."

Drifter leaped after Smiles and caught his wrist while the man's arm was still bent up by his chest with the Bulldog revolver just free of his lapel. Drifter jerked the arm sideways, twisting Smiles halfway around and cracking the wrist on the balcony rail. Smiles cried out with pain, and the gun went off and dropped from his fingers. Drifter threw him on around till he was facing toward the stairs and booted him in the behind with a knee. Smiles stumbled forward, trying to keep from falling, and then sprawled headlong on the flowered carpet. He had only risen to his hands and knees before Drifter was on him again, pulling him up by the collar and twisting him around and booting him down the stairs with that knee again.

Smiles did a somersault and bounced on down. Halfway to the bottom, he reached out and caught one of the spindles, jerking to a stop. He pulled himself up by the rail, tears of utter rage streaming from his face, and flung himself back up at Drifter, screaming hoarsely. A woman's voice sounded sharply over Smiles's yells.

"Drifter! Stop it, you fools! Drifter!"

The two men met with a dull, fleshy sound. Drifter had been coming from above, and his greater momentum carried Smiles back down the stairs, smashing into the railing. The rail collapsed with a splintering crash, and both men tumbled through. Poker jumped back from his lay-out below as Smiles fell into the table, scattering chips and cards, and then Drifter came down on top of Smiles. The table gave way beneath their weight, breaking in the center and dumping them on the floor.

Smiles struggled up from beneath Drifter, wrenching one of the broken table legs loose. Drifter tried to dodge the blow, but the banker's box caught his shoulder, and the table leg slammed into his head. Smiles got up, slugging with the leg again. Drifter rolled desperately, catching that blow on his back, trying to get out from beneath the box. Smiles followed him, bloody face twisted, snarling insanely, beating at him with that leg. The room spun before Drifter, and he fell over sideways against the stairway when he tried to rise.

"Smiles!" screamed Faye from somewhere above. "Stop it!"

Smiles knocked Drifter back into a corner with another blow and leaped on in to finish it. Huddled there with his back against the wall beneath the balcony, Drifter drew his knees into his stomach and took another blow in the face to let Smiles come up against him, and then straightened his legs violently.

Smiles flew backward, crashing into the mess of the broken table again. Drifter jumped away from the wall, staggering dizzily after the man. Panting gustily, he caught Smiles by the shirt collar and jerked him up off the poker lay-out, giving him an open-handed slap that jerked his head halfway around, coming back with a backhand blow that knocked his head the other way. Holding him like that, and hitting him, first one side, then the other, Drifter drove him back across the room, knocking over a chair by the roulette table.

Smiles couldn't get any leverage to fight back until he stumbled into the bar. Then he straightened, driving a blow into Drifter's stomach. Drifter gasped at the pain, bellying in hard against Smiles, but it had loosened his grip on the man long enough for Smiles to twist around, kicking Drifter away, and claw over the bar.

Smiles dropped on the other side and grabbed for one of the bottles on the shelf. Drifter was on top of the bar when Smiles turned, and he jumped the man with both spike heels right in his face. Smiles fell back against the wall with a broken cry, arm sweeping spasmodically across the shelf and knocking a whole row of bottles down to fill the room with their glass-breaking crash.

Slipping on the broken glass and flowing liquor, Drifter

pulled Smiles up again. Smiles still held that one bottle, broken off at the bottom now, and he tried to jam it into Drifter's face. Drifter caught the wrist and twisted it, and Smiles shouted hoarsely with the pain, and dropped the bottle. Then, bellied up against the man once more, Drifter began hitting him that way again. Smiles couldn't go back any farther, and he jerked from one side to the other under the blows, screaming in rage and pain. Then his screams became choked sobs. Finally the sounds he made were hardly audible, or human, and he sagged against Drifter.

Drifter hit him a last backhand blow across his wrecked face, then let go his collar, stepping back. The broken bottles covering the floor made a tinkling protest as Smiles slid down into them.

Drifter wiped a bloody hand across his mouth, drawing a shuddering breath. "I told you that little habit of yours would irritate somebody, someday."

VI

The latest rage in chandeliers was one entirely of steel, with medallions of Dutch ware called faience, and the Silver Slipper boasted four of these, each containing a hundred gilt candles that cast their light over all the noise and confusion Custer Street could pack into the huge lower hall. Peter Poker was busy at his table and six bartenders sweated behind the longest strip of mahogany in Laramie and the muted slap of cards and chips from the tables at the rear mingled with the incessant *click* of the roulette wheel to form an undertone beneath the constant mutter of voices.

"Place your bets, ladies and gentlemen. All bets down before the wheel starts spinning. Place your bets."

"Keno. Seven, eight, nine. Keno."

"Full house. Beat it?"

"Table stakes here, friend."

"Rye and chaser."

There was a long line cashing in chips at the grille near the front door, and Faye stood there, giving that warm, personal smile to every man who came through the batwings, casting him instantly under her spell. The sequins on her green velvet gown flared and died and flared again with her every movement, shimmering for an instant across the curve of her hip as she turned so the light fell on them there, then blinking out as she turned the other way, and glittering into life across the swell of her bosom as the light struck them there. Moving toward the front door, Drifter heard her laugh float up over the other sounds like the cool tintinnabulation of ice in a glass. She saw him, and moved back toward the Chinese screen flanking the grille, smiling away the men who would have followed.

"You can turn it off and on like a faucet, can't you?" said Drifter.

They were alone now, behind the screen. "What?"

"The charm," he said. "You use it like Peter Poker uses his cards. He can pull an ace whenever he wants. At his table, he's king, and he glories in it. Like you glory in this. Is that the pull it has for you, Faye? The sense of power it gives you? Twisting those poor devils around your little finger with a smile and watching them lose all their money on your tables and then brushing them off?"

"Why not?" Her eyes held a strange glitter. "Maybe some people need power and others need food. It satisfies something inside me, Drifter. I rule the Slipper and I rule Laramie and I'll rule all of Wyoming Territory before I'm through."

"And what will you have when you are through, Faye?"

For a moment, her face softened. "What will you have, Drifter?"

"Nothing," he said. "That's what I mean, Faye. We're both kidding ourselves. We're both riding a lonely trail and trying to tell ourselves it's what we want. Does this really satisfy you, Faye? A woman needs more than power. You showed me you weren't any different than any other woman, up in your room the other morning."

She stiffened. "I told you we'd forget that."

"Can you forget it?" he said. "I can't. You didn't tell me to get out because you were mad. You were afraid. Afraid of yourself, Faye. You said no man ever did that to you. What you meant was you'd never let any man see what you were really like before. When this job is over, Faye, get out of it with me. I know a little spread up in the Bighorns I could get. . . ."

She had begun to tremble perceptibly again with the same emotion that had shaken her up in the room the other day, and he knew what it was now. "No, Drifter, no! You and I aren't for each other. You know what kind of a woman I am. . . ."

"And that's exactly why you're the only woman I ever said this to," he told her. "I'm not a kid, like Dean Remington, Faye. I don't come to you with a sparkler. I know you can have all those you want. And I know that isn't what you want, really. I don't wear Sunday school pants myself, Faye. I've got mud on my boots that won't come off."

She backed away from him, unable to meet his eyes. "I said we'd forget it. This is the last time you'll talk this way, Drifter, understand? You'd better go now. Here comes Smiles. He'll never forgive you for what you did the other day. It would have been better to meet him with a gun. Slapping him around like that. . . ."

His shoulders sagged wearily. "I did that on purpose. It

usually puts things good and straight in a man's mind. I told you I never used an iron unless there was no other way out."

"All right. All right. You're going out again tonight? Kappas is at the cabin."

He nodded, and left her standing there, feeling very tired suddenly. Outside, he got his bay and turned west on Custer. The row of oil lamps lining the gaudy façade of the Silver Slipper reminded him of the sequins on Faye's gown somehow, flaring and dying and flaring again, the brightest thing on Gambler's Row.

It was close to dawn when he reached the ridge in the Medicine Bows, hitching his horse in timber on the far side. Georgie Kappas was hunkered down among the rocks above the shack, narrow face lined with fatigue. Drifter slid down through the talus.

"Anything?"

Kappas shook his head. "Nothing. I spent some time trying to track them away from the cabin, but the trail's cold, and I lost it where you did when it hit water about a mile below the saddle. This is crazy, Drifter."

"If they left Albert Afton here for a purpose last time," said Drifter, "they'll want to know what's happened to him. And whoever it was lit out in such a hurry left a lot of truck in the shack. There wasn't anything I could identify anybody by, but they won't be sure of that, and they'll begin to wonder, and sooner or later they'll be coming back."

"You think it's Kings Nixon?"

"Yeah," said Drifter, and his eyes narrowed at the man, "Nixon. Faye sent you out here to help me ever since I refused to kill Nixon for her. Is that what you're supposed to take care of if we meet Kings out here, Georgie?"

"She told me you wouldn't gun Nixon," said Kappas.

★ ★ ★ ★ ★

Kappas slept a while, and Drifter leaned back against the rocks, watching the cabin below. This was the fifth day of waiting up here, and he could feel the thin bite of impatience at his loins when he thought of that.

Maybe it was noon when the man appeared out of the scrub pine on the far side of the cabin. If Drifter had done it, he would have made a circuit of the ridges above the shack, but this man was apparently satisfied with staking his horse farther back and then waiting there at the fringe of timber for a few moments to see if he could spot any movement. He stepped out with a Winchester hooked in an elbow. Drifter let the man get inside the shack, then shook Kappas, with his hand over his mouth.

They hadn't reached the cabin before smoke began rising from the tin-pipe chimney. Drifter had left the truck scattered around the room the way he had found it, and the man had piled this in front of the wood stove and was stuffing it piece by piece into the fire.

"When you drop that," said Drifter, "don't pick up anything else."

The man whirled with a gasp, still gripping the high-heeled boot he had been going to put in the stove. He made a jerky move toward his Winchester, leaning against the plank table, then he dropped the boot, straightening, his face pale. Kappas got around in front of Drifter, looking intently at the man.

"Who is he?" said Drifter.

"Edward Lederer," said Kappas.

"That leaves us one, then," said Drifter, and his voice was husky and strangely forced. Still holding his Rogers and Spencer on the man, he moved in. "Where is he?"

"Who?" said the other.

71

"You're Edward Lederer?" Drifter's narrowed eyes had become clouded, as if swept by the acrid gray powder of a fired gun. "And Albert Afton is outside beneath a pile of rocks. Dean Remington. Where is he?"

There wasn't much character in Lederer's receding chin and watery blue eyes, and his fear was plain in the putty color of his sagging jowls. "I don't know what you're talking about."

Drifter read the weakness in the man, and it was what he used. He put his own gun away and stepped in close, grabbing Lederer by the lapels of his blue coat. All the ease went out of Drifter's big body, and the line of his shoulders took on a new breadth. His voice held an ineffable threat in its low, strained tones.

"Listen," he said between his teeth. "Have you ever been pistol-whipped? Down in Texas they whip the flesh off a man's face in strips and sun-cure it and tie it together for dally ropes. That's what I'm going to do with you unless you talk up, and fast. You'd be surprised how much of your face I could take off and still leave you conscious enough to feel the pain."

Lederer choked on his breath. "OK, OK, cut it out, will you, lemme go. Kings sent me to find out what had happened to Afton, that's all, and to burn whatever we'd left in the shack. Nixon knew you were leaving town every day and tried to have Mike trail you, but you lost yourself every time. They thought you was tracking, anyway. Couldn't figure anybody had the patience to squat on an empty cabin this long."

Drifter shoved him over against the wall hard enough to shake the whole structure, almost shouting: "I don't mean that! Where've you got the kid? You want me to reach for my gun?"

"No," gasped Lederer. "Don't. No. We've got Remington

over in the Italian Caves. Been keeping him there ever since we left here."

"Italian Caves?" said Drifter.

They were farther into the Medicine Bows where the snow never melted on the peaks, and the pine cones set up a ghostly crackle beneath the horse's hoofs that echoed somberly down the lanes of dark timber. It had been a long ride, and Drifter stepped stiffly off his bay where they had halted in the trees. From here, they could see three animals hitched in front of the cave mouth, one of them unsaddled. The little muscles around Drifter's mouth had begun to twitch, and he was breathing heavily. He jammed his gun into Lederer.

"Any guards?"

Lederer nodded a nervous head down past the horses toward a motte of juniper. "One down there with a Ward-Burton."

"I ought to shoot you for that," said Drifter viciously. He waved his gun at the trees above the cave. "There's high ground. If there's a guard, he'll be there. We'll give you time to work above the timber there, Kappas, then we'll move into the open. Whatever it draws from the guard, it'll show you where he is, and you can do whatever's necessary after that."

Kappas nodded, and walked his horse off through the trees. The gun was trembling in Drifter's hand now. He didn't think he could hold himself in much longer. He had come so far for this. Finally he nudged the putty-faced Lederer.

"This iron is going to be in your back. If the guard hails you, tell him Nixon sent a new man with you. If he starts shooting, you can go ahead and run wherever you want."

They moved away from the trees and were about half the distance to the cave when a man appeared in the growth

73

above the cave. "Who's that with you, Ed?"

Drifter was close behind Lederer, and his gun wasn't evident to the man above. He felt Lederer's body grow rigid as he answered. "New man. Nixon sent. . . ."

The shot cut him off. The man above stiffened, then pitched face downward to disappear in the wild green hops. Kappas came jumping down through the scrub pine behind him.

"I got him!" he shouted.

Drifter heard Kappas only dimly, because whoever was inside would have heard the shot, and he had already given Lederer a hard shove and was running for the cave. A man came out of the cave with a Ward-Burton bolt action across his belly.

"Kerry?" he shouted.

"Here's that bronc' you didn't peel!" Drifter screamed at him. "This is your last throw." He shot, and shot again, still going forward.

The bullet caught Tie-Down Brown in his stomach right above his tightly held gun, and he went down at a run, hand twitching futilely at the Ward-Burton's bolt.

It was all black before Drifter inside the cave, and he stumbled over something and went headlong, and scrambled erect, shouting: "Dean, Dean, you in here?"

"Drifter! How did you tie onto this?"

Drifter's eyes were accustomed to the gloom now. He got to the young man, lying bound hand and foot on the blanket behind the litter of tin cans and boxes, and ripped at the lashings. He had the boy's hands undone when Kappas came into the cave, stopping a moment until he could see.

"That him?"

"Yeah," said Drifter, going for Dean's ankles. He was bent

over them when the shot deafened him. He whirled around, and for a moment couldn't comprehend it—Kappas, standing there with the smoking gun in his hand. Dean's face was stamped with the agony. Then it swept over Drifter: he heard someone screaming—"That's why she sent you here,"—and realized it was himself—"to kill him, not to kill Nixon, to kill *him!*" Then he didn't know anything more until Dean's call came through the haze from somewhere far off.

"Drifter, Drifter . . . !"

He heard a spasmodic grunt after that, and it was the way he came out of it, still grunting every time he hit Kappas's black head against the ground. He was straddling the man, hands still twined in Kappas's hair. He rose shakily, leaving Kappas lying limp and bloody there, and turned back to the boy.

"Drifter," said Remington again, "I guess . . . I guess you rounded up a lot of cows for nothing. . . ."

Drifter went to his knees beside the boy, staring dazedly at the bloody hole in Dean's chest. "She sent Kappas for you," he said. "Not for Nixon. You . . . oh, damn her, I'll kill her for this, kid, I swear I will. Oh, damn her, damn her, damn her. . . ."

"Faye?" The boy's face was white. "Don't blame her, Drifter. I caused her enough trouble. I caused everybody trouble. Even you. A fine brother I turned to be. How did you tie onto it?"

"I heard you were working in Laramie and sent you a letter in care of Hackett's Livery," said Drifter, and he was sobbing unashamedly now. "They sent it back with another note, saying you'd left suddenly. I knew you'd meant to settle down here, Dean, so I thought that sounded fishy. All the way down from Montana, I kept looking up old friends to see if they'd heard anything of you. In Cheyenne, I met Kappas, and he said Faye Warren was looking for a man down here. I thought it would be the easiest way to get on the inside of things. The second day after I hired out to her, I found you were mixed up in this somehow. I'll get her for it, kid. I swear I will."

He tried to lift the boy, but Dean gasped. "No, Drifter. The fence is down for good. Just these last few minutes. I haven't seen as much of you as I'd like lately. Always realize things like that too late, don't you? Fine brother I turned out to be. . . ."

"Don't be crazy. I'm the drifter. You were always the steady boy, Dean. How did you get mixed up in this? You saw who killed Gerald Pine?"

"Yes," said the boy weakly. "That night, I'd tried to give the ring to Faye and she'd refused it. Treated me like a little boy. Maybe I was a little boy. I left her place, meaning to get out of town, paid my rent up, told Hackett I was through, got my horse. Feeling so low I stopped at Banner's for a drink. Took too many, I guess. Ended up on Rot-Gut End somewhere. Maybe it was Lazy Ike's they tossed me out of. Must have been about four in the morning. Custer deserted. On the intersection at Second I saw Pine come out of the Cosmopolitan Hotel. I saw it all right there, Drifter, the whole thing . . ."—Dean coughed faintly, choked—"the whole dirty thing. Kings Nixon was the first one out on Custer after the shot. He must have realized I was the only witness, must have realized what my knowledge could mean to him if he used it right. Asked me if I'd seen who killed Pine. . . ."

"You didn't tell him?"

"I was all fogged up with red-eye, Drifter. I told him I had. Didn't tell him who it was, understand. Just what I'd seen. Then I realized the mistake I'd made and clammed up. Kings brought me to that cabin first. They worked me over every day, trying to make me tell. Then Nixon came up and rushed me off to the caves. Said you were getting too warm. I guess you were the one who shot Afton at the shack? Both Lederer and Afton worked for Kings. Kings killed two birds with one stone by having them disappear from Laramie. That way, whoever was running things on the Row wouldn't know for sure just who the witness was until Kings chose to make his move."

"They worked you over. Did you . . . ?"

"No," gasped Dean. "I never told them who killed Pine. Think I would. Think I'd tell anybody? Only you, Drifter."

"Then . . . who?"

"It took a big person to do it, Drifter." Dean's voice was barely audible. "Not Banner or Nixon or Lazy Ike. They wouldn't put their heads in a noose by killing the brother of a federal judge. Not Smiles, either, or Kappas. Kappas had just slipped one U.S. marshal down in Texas. He was too smart to make that mistake again. He'd gun Nixon or you or me, Drifter, but not Pine. It took a larger person than any of them to kill Gerald Pine, the biggest person in Laramie."

Drifter felt himself grow rigid. "Dean, you don't mean . . . ?"

"I do," choked Dean Remington, and said the last thing he would ever say: "Faye Warren."

VII

The bay horse collapsed beneath Drifter just beyond the sheds of the Laramie North Park and Central, and he jumped off as it went down, running on across the first set of tracks, sweat blinding him. His whole being seemed consumed by the leaping flame of an unutterable rage at Faye Warren. She had killed his brother just as surely as if she had pulled the trigger on Kappas's gun, and Drifter's one implacable desire was to see her dead for it. He didn't think of her as a woman any more. He didn't think any more. He was filled with that terrible, bestial rage, wiping all sane thought from him, sending him across the gleaming rails in a dead run without feeling the exhaustion of the long ride or the pain of his wounds or anything.

Kappas must have come to in time to hear Dean tell who Pines's murderer was. Drifter had a hazy memory of Kappas, jumping him from the corner of the cave, bloody face twisted, gun coming down. The blow of the bullet had stunned Drifter, and all he had been able to do was grapple with Kappas, forcing the man's weapon out between them as it went off. He had wrenched the gun free after that, but Kappas had fought himself away, and Drifter had lost him in the gloom of the cave. When he had turned back to his brother, Dean had been dead.

Drifter ran past the roundhouse now, and into shanty town, past the Brady rooming house. Then he could see across the Union Pacific tracks to Custer Street where it terminated in Rot-Gut End. The thin early evening crowd made a nervous shift in the falling dusk. Someone ran out of the Full House. Kings Nixon?

"Drifter!" he shouted, and must have been the first to see Drifter coming at a dogged run across the tracks, because the others in the street turned, and then shoved hurriedly to either side, ducking into the Full House or Lazy Ike's, bunching up along the sidewalk. Only Nixon remained in the street now, and he shouted again. "Don't be a fool, Drifter! Kappas reached the Row half an hour ago! We all know about it! You'll never get to Faye! You'll have to go through every man on Custer Street to do it, and you'll never get to her!"

"I thought you were bucking Faye's bank!" shouted

Drifter, running across the Union Pacific tracks and into Custer.

"We fight each other enough," said Nixon, "but when anything threatens the Row from inside, we're all sitting on the same side of the lay-out, Drifter."

Nixon did something with his cane, and the long shaft of it dropped to the ground, leaving the gold head in the man's hand. Drifter realized what it was too late, and saw he could never make it raising his gun. The two weapons crashed simultaneously, but the Derringer which had been fitted into the top of the cane went off into the air because Nixon was already falling backward. Drifter ran past his body, still holding the Rogers and Spencer where he had shot from the hip.

Drifter reached Second Street. He was out of Rot-Gut End now, and going into the second block of the Row. Tight little groups stood along the walk and in the doors, watching him.

"Drifter?" shouted somebody from ahead. "Don't be a fool! Go back, Drifter . . . !"

It was Jigger's Irish voice. Banner's head barman stood in the middle of the street, his white coat gleaming dimly in the gloom.

"I'm coming, Jigger!" yelled Drifter savagely, and his figure made a tall, swaying, pounding shadow in the dusk, going straight down the center of Custer. "Get out of my way."

"I don't want to do it, Drifter!" shouted Jigger, and there was something desperate in his voice. "You were the best customer I had. I don't want to do it!"

Then he must have seen how useless it was, and he began shooting. With that white coat for his target, Drifter fired. The men on the sidewalk opened up then, and Custer rocked to the bedlam of sound. Drifter didn't know when the bullet caught him in the leg, or when Jigger went down. He stumbled on through the dark one or two more steps, unable to see Jigger's white blot before him any more, emptying his gun at the men on the left side, then tripped over someone, and fell on his face.

It was Jigger, lying there, still holding his Winchester. Sprawled on the man, Drifter jammed his empty six-gun back in its leather and pulled the carbine from beneath Jigger.

"Did you get him?" shouted Banner, his boots clattering down the walk on the right side—"Drifter?"—and then he must have seen Drifter's shift out in the street, because he stopped.

"No, Orin, they didn't get me," said Drifter, and drove his first shot at Banner. They began firing from across the way again, and Banner jumped forward off the boardwalk, trying to keep himself from falling so he could shoot at Drifter, and then Drifter put a second slug into him, and Banner fell on his face in the wheel ruts by the curb.

The Silver Slipper was farther up Custer, on the opposite side from Banner's, and Drifter understood what they were waiting for. The flickering oil lamps lining the gaudy façade of the Slipper were the brightest lights on Custer, casting their illumination clear across the street, and Drifter couldn't move any farther without being clearly revealed by them.

When he got to his knees with Jigger's Winchester, he began crawling up the middle of the street, and firing deliberately at the lights on the Slipper.

Peter Poker's striped shirt showed for a moment in the yellow glow, and his voice came to Drifter hoarsely. "Get him before he does that, damn you! Get Drifter before he shoots out those lights."

"If you want to try it," yelled someone from the darkness, "go ahead!"

Drifter turned and threw his last shot at a man who had been trying to get in from behind, driving him back. He picked up the hot ejected cartridge in his fingers, measuring it blindly. .44? It was a chance. His Rogers and Spencer was a .44. He thumbed a fresh shell from his cartridge belt and started reloading the Winchester.

"Get him!" screamed Peter Poker.

The pound of Drifter's Winchester drowned him out, and the fourth lamp crashed down from the façade, throwing a stream of burning oil over the horses tied at the hitch rack and sending them into a kicking, squealing frenzy.

One of them broke loose and galloped past Drifter. Choking in its dust, Drifter shot out another lamp. More men were moving in from behind now, their lead searching him out in all that darkness, and he knew he couldn't wait any longer. He snapped the carbine's lever and drove a shot at the final lamp, and then got to his feet.

He had saved his wounded leg for this last, and he went forward in a lopsided run, sobbing with agony every time his weight came down on the right leg. In the darkness beneath the Slipper's façade, he could still hear the horses fighting, and he threw himself toward them, falling against the first one and catching at its rig to keep from going down.

"Where is he?" shouted Poker.

"Over there!" yelled a man from behind Drifter. "In the horses!"

They were bunching up across the sidewalk in front of the Slipper's batwings now, and coming in from behind him, their guns sending the horses into another frenzy. Drifter tore the reins of the nigh animal loose and hauled himself into the saddle, still holding the Winchester. The spooked mount whirled out into the middle of the street, heaving and kicking.

Drifter bunched the reins in one hand and fought it

around toward the saloon again, then kicked it hard in the flanks. The animal screamed and bolted straight for the hitch rack. Drifter felt the rack crash beneath him as the horse went through it, clattering up onto the boardwalk.

The men before the doors scattered from the charging beast. Peter Poker didn't make it in time, and the animal carried him right on through to the inside, along with the batwings it had torn loose, and then trampled him under.

Hat ripped off by the top of the door, Drifter drove the squalling animal right through the crowd in the bottom hall, beating them aside with his Winchester, smashing the faro lay-out, careening off the roulette table. At the foot of the stairs, the horse stumbled and went into the railing. Drifter jumped off before it went down, stumbling halfway up the stairs before his bad leg gave out beneath him.

He grabbed at the smashed railing, hauling himself erect, pulling himself on up the stairs. A houseman fought free of the milling, shouting crowd below, jumping around the madly kicking horse, taking the first step up after Drifter with a six-shooter. At the head of the stairs, Drifter turned, leaning against the rail. Then the houseman stopped, looking up past Drifter.

"All right, Dirk," said Smiles. "We'll take care of him."

They stood in the doorway of Faye's apartment down at the end of the balcony: Smiles, big and square and solid with his derby hat tilted back and his stogie poking from one corner of his mouth, Georgie Kappas, face still bloody from Drifter's beating.

"I didn't think you'd get this far," said Smiles, and his bottle green lapel was shoved back to hook a thumb in the armhole of his vest.

"Coming the rest of the way?" said Kappas, and pushed the tails of his torn claw hammer back off the butt of his gun.

"I'm coming," gasped Drifter, and lurched away from the rail, and saw Kappas crouch and dive, and saw Smiles unhook his thumb from his vest and reach beneath his coat, and knew that whichever one he shot, the other would get him, so he didn't shoot. Grabbing the Winchester in both hands so it was lengthwise across his body, he heaved it at them, and ran in after it.

The balcony wasn't very wide, and the two men were standing close enough together so that the carbine took them both, butt smashing into the hand Smiles was pulling from beneath his coat, barrel hitting Kappas across the face. Drifter struck them after that, as Smiles's gun went off at the roof, knocked upward by the carbine butt.

Drifter's weight carried them both back against the door, and it swung inward, and all three men hurtled into the room. Kappas had his gun out, twisting beneath Drifter and Smiles to fire.

Drifter grabbed the weapon in both hands, jerking it into Smiles. It went off that way, and Smiles stiffened beneath Drifter, and collapsed. Drifter twisted the gun on around until Kappas screamed and let go. Kappas tried to roll out from beneath Smiles's limp body. Drifter caught him while he was belly-down. The blow drove Kappa's face into the Brussels carpet with a soft, dull sound. Drifter was still sprawled across the two men when the muffled shot came from Faye's boudoir. A strange silence followed, and all the heat of rage was driven from Drifter suddenly.

He had to hang on the door of the boudoir when he opened it, and swung in on the knob, and almost fell again. Judge Herman Pine stood in the middle of the sumptuous apartment with a smoking Colt in his hand, a dull glaze in his eyes, the haggard, driven lines of his face suddenly weary and gaunt and spent.

"Go ahead," he said. "Kill me. I've done what I came to do. I got word Kappas had hit Laramie with news that the witness was out of the way. I knew our last chance of avenging my brother's death that way was gone. I should have known this was the only way from the beginning. Go ahead. I'm a murderer now, just like the rest of you, and my brother's avenged, and you can kill me. . . ."

Drifter had reached Faye by then, lifting her onto the richly tufted four-poster bed. Already red blood was seeping from beneath her gown.

"You said you'd tear my town apart with your bare hands, didn't you?" She laughed. Then she drew a sharp breath, and the agony crossed her face. "Kappas was in such a hurry to tell me you were coming that he left the bottom door to those back stairs open. That's how Pine got in. Too bad he beat you to the draw."

"I couldn't have done it, anyway," said Drifter. "I meant to . . . all the way in I meant to . . . but no matter what you did, I know now I wouldn't have done it, Faye."

"Kappas said Remington was your brother," she murmured weakly. "Afton knew that? I thought it would take more than surprise to make him pull on you there at the shack."

"I'd known Afton in Kansas," said Drifter. "When he saw me there at the shack, he knew I'd come for my brother, and that there was only one thing would stop me, and he tried that. Faye . . . Dean told me who killed Gerald Pine."

She nodded weakly. "Pine sent word he wanted to see me at the Cosmopolitan Hotel. After the Slipper closed that night, I met him in the room he'd taken. He said he'd found out I was the brains behind the Row. He knew trying to wipe out the Row the way he was doing would take a big fight, and he offered me a compromise. He'd let me pull out with my cash, and wouldn't bring charges against me personally or expose my connection with the machine here. My leaving would cripple the machine so he wouldn't have any trouble finishing the Row. I refused him and tried to leave. He followed me down the back stairs to Third, still arguing. No one had seen us up to then. He got hot under the collar when I kept refusing. He put his hands on me, Drifter. I told you I'd never let a man do that. . . ."

Pine was staring at her stupidly. "You . . . you . . . ?"

"Yes, Judge." Faye laughed weakly. "You were more correct than you realized when you came here with that gun."

"But I didn't realize," said Pine dazedly. "I had no idea. I was too crazy to think, I guess. I only came here because it seemed the logical place. You were the one who'd taken those chits, the one I'd dealt with. My brother. You were the one. . . ."

"And my brother," said Drifter. "If you'd known who Dean really was, Faye, would you still have sent Kappas out to kill him?"

"Yes," she said. "I loved you, Drifter. You were right when you said I hadn't shown myself to any other man that way. You were right when you said I told you to get out because I was afraid. Afraid of myself, Drifter. Afraid it would mean the finish of everything here if I let myself go. But loving you, if you'd gotten in my way, I would have put you out of it, just like I did your brother. Can you understand that, Drifter?"

"I guess I can, Faye," he said dully. "I guess it's the kind you are. I could see what kind you were from the first, and I must have known just about how you'd deal your cards if things turned out this way. And still I couldn't help how I felt about you."

"You know," she murmured, "in a way I would have liked to see that little spread in the Bighorns you told me about. . . ."

He caught her hand. "Faye?"

Brush Buster

Les Savage, Jr., completed this short novel in April,
1948 and titled it "Brush Buster." It was submitted at
once to Malcolm Reiss who was general fiction editor
for the Fiction House magazines. Reiss bought it on
May 4, 1948, paying the author $375.00. It appeared
under the title "Beware the Six-Gun Saint" in *Lariat
Story Magazine* (11/48). For its first publication in
book form the author's original title has been restored.

I

There was a horse the color of powder smoke hitched to the
tie rack in front of the Lamar house. Sight of it did not help
the anger in Nolan Moore as he emerged from the brush.
Then he saw the cowhide hung on the corral fence behind the
house, with a Bootjack brand on its hip. He scowled viciously, and dismounted.

He took a hitch with the reins around a mesquite branch,
and walked to the house. He was a short, compact man,
hardly average height, even with the added three inches of
heel on his Coffeyville boots. He wore the rawhide leggings
called *chivarras* in this Texas brush-land so near the Mexican
border. His ducking jacket was rawhide, too, dark with age

except where the worn places across the back and elbows had whitened it.

The front door swung ajar, and there was nobody within the dank, crude interior of the two-room mud *jacal*. He walked past the open door and around the corner of the *jacal* and almost stepped into Ivory Lamar and Lee Daggett, locked in a tight embrace. Ivory tore free of Daggett, flushing deeply.

"Next time I'll wear a cowbell," said Moore, hiding his own emotion beneath the biting acidity of his voice.

"Someday I'm going to knock that salt out of you," said Daggett.

"Nobody's standing on your shirt tail," Moore told him.

"Oh, stop it," Ivory said hotly. "What do you want, Nolan?"

She had the deep-breasted, full-bodied lushness of her Mexican heritage, but girlhood spent in an American convent had left little accent to her English. Her hair was blue-black as a Colt barrel, her eyes were green as jade, and her lips held a petulant, crimson richness that had always tantalized Moore. It was an effort to keep his anger before the poignancy she always brought to him.

"I came to tell your father he'd better stop butchering my beef," he said.

"Seems to me being a cattleman is making you forget things, Moore," said Daggett.

Moore let his eyes pass to the man. Daggett was half a head taller, with a sway-backed stance that gave him a perpetual swagger, afoot or a-horse, a certain tensile threat to the line of his long, lean body in its sheath of suede *charro* pants and rawhide ducking jacket. The grueling exigencies of this brush country had scored and hardened his long, reckless face, giving him a vague sense of past suffering that could appeal to a woman. There was heritage of Satan in the shaggy peak of his sun-bleached brows, and no depth to his eyes, only silvery, opaque surfaces that glittered blank as ice when the light caught them right.

"What have I forgotten?" Moore asked him.

"It's always been a custom of the country to let a man butcher a steer running any brand, just so long as he eats it, and doesn't try to hide the fact."

"That's right," said Ivory. "Your steer hide is in plain sight on our corral."

Moore turned to her, a plea entering his voice. "You know the combination of this butchering and the rustling has already broken three men on the Bootjack, Ivory. . . ."

"Only a fool would mortgage his soul away for that greasy-sack outfit anyway," said Ivory contemptuously. "How long did you work for Warren's Double Fork to get that stake? Five years? And before that, most of your life? Eating dust on some other man's trail herd. Jolting the guts out of you on another man's bronc's. And what have you got to show for it? Nothing but a pot-rack outfit with a cow-pen herd that isn't even big enough to feed a few butchers."

His black eyes grew somber. His voice was barely audible. "I didn't think you'd look at it that way."

Ivory tossed her head. "You know what I think about breaking your back all your life for beans. I've seen too much of it. My mother wasn't any different from you, and she worked herself to death. Ninety percent of the men who try it the way you are have ended up out here in the brush with no more than dirty rawhide on their backs. You've seen them, Nolan. Old before their time. Only knowing one thing in the world . . . brush popping . . . and unable to do that because they're so busted up from doing it in the past they can't even sit a horse. Beaten and battered by the thickets till their bodies are covered with lumps and their internal injuries are killing them."

Moore did not actually look at Daggett. "Maybe you'd rather have a man earn his money other ways, Ivory."

"You aren't getting personal, are you, Moore?" Daggett asked.

"Let him, Lee," Ivory said defiantly. "Maybe I would, Nolan. Maybe I'd rather have a man use his head a little. Dad never did a day's work in his life, and he's better off than you."

"I don't recall Daggett ever worked much, either. . . ."

"He's still better off than you . . . throw in the Bootjack, and he's still better off," flamed Ivory.

"If you call riding around on a silver-plated Mexican tree kak and a smoke-colored prairie lawyer he calls a horse. . . ."

Daggett's long body inclined sharply toward Moore. "What's wrong with my horse?"

"Nothing that would keep him from the crows," said Moore. "A whole rail full of Mexican kaks wouldn't hide that nigger branding you done on his back. How do you sit a saddle so heavy? No wonder he cuts himself up so much on the brush."

"He'll bust any thicket your sop-and-taters nag, Hokey Pokey, will," Daggett said irately.

"With quarters like that?" scoffed Moore. "He hasn't got enough bulge in his rump to push him through a heavy fog, much less a thicket."

"Stop it," Ivory told them.

"Only a cold-blooded hack like your hammer-headed navvy would pack so much tallow on his rump!" Daggett was shouting now.

"I wouldn't have hot blood in this brush," said Moore. "Get an Arab like Smoke het up and he won't even see the thicket he's going at. Is that how you got all those thoroughpins on his hocks? I never saw a horse with so many bog spavins."

"I asked you to stop it!" Ivory cried. She stopped then, bosom heaving, and turned her hot gaze on Moore. "You'll have to come back later for Dad."

"You can save me the trouble," said Moore. "Just tell him I'm shooting on sight the next time I catch anybody butchering my beef."

The blood drained from her face. "Nolan! You don't mean that."

"I do. I've tried every other way, and you know it. I've asked them to stop it a dozen times, your father included. They know the Bootjack can't stand the drain. I've tried getting Sheriff Kynette to help me. He hasn't been to the Bootjack since I took over. I choused a pair of butchers into town and preferred charges and found them riding free as birds the next day. I'm through taking it easy on this bronc', Ivory. The next time I snub up, it's going to hurt."

"And while you're killing a few innocent men, the rustlers are still stealing you blind! Get off my land, Nolan!"

"I've always thought I might find the butchers and the rustlers in the same pasture," said Moore.

Ivory's eyes widened till they looked like wet, black pools, then narrowed till he could hardly see them between the lids. "I won't take any more," she said, although her lips barely moved. "Get out, Nolan, before I have you thrown out."

"I don't see anyone to do it," he said dryly.

"Look this way," said Daggett, grabbing Moore's elbow and spinning him halfway around. "Now get out, Moore. . . ."

"Not with your hands on me," said Moore, and let all the bitter, frustrating, pent-up anger of months explode in his whirling motion back toward Daggett, in the blow he drove at the man's belly. Daggett grunted and was knocked against the wall so hard the adobe cracked. Face contorted, Daggett pushed himself off the wall.

Moore ducked in under his swing and caught him in the stomach with a second punch. Daggett made another spasmodic sound of pain, folding over the fist to grab for Moore's shoulder. Moore shifted to his other foot and pulled the left back for a short inside blow. It was as vicious and calculated as the other two had been, and it finished Daggett. He went back against the wall again, and slid to the ground. Huddled over there, he made an effort to rise, and failed, emitting a faint, defeated, retching sound. Moore picked his hat off the earth and dusted it against one leg with a vindictive slap.

"It's about time somebody took me at my word," he said. "I told you it would hurt the next time I snubbed up."

II

Range delivery meant that the buyer inspected the seller's ranch and paid for what the seller purported to own—and then went out and tried to find it. This was the way most spreads were bought in a country where the brush was so thick it would take a dozen full crews five years to find out how many cows any given outfit actually ran. This was the way Moore had bought the Bootjack.

It was the usual policy to have a fair estimate of the seller's integrity, or of the number of beeves his pasture held, and having worked in the vicinity the last five years Moore had known about what to expect. There were enough cattle in those thickets to make it a good spread if the rustling could be stopped. Running right up to the Río Grande, with half of its acreage made up of brush so thick it had never been explored, it was a ripe plum for the border hoppers. The brand had been recorded in Webb County for fifteen years when the third man to own the property was ready to give up. When Moore heard the ridiculously low figure that was being asked, he dug out every last dollar he had saved during his five years on the Double Fork in order to make a down payment.

It had left him so broke he couldn't hire a crew yet. But he had expected to round up enough animals by himself to meet the payments and lay aside enough for a crew next year. It was working on a pretty thin shoestring, but he was thirty-five now, and he looked upon this as just about the last chance for a man who had labored all his life for other men and had dreamed all his life of being his own master.

The day after returning from the Lamar place, he got his horse and a pair of neck oxen and started on his lone roundup again. He couldn't spend all his time chasing rustlers and butchers. He still kept thinking of Ivory in Daggett's arms, and feeling sick every time he thought of it. He and Daggett had both been hanging around the Lamar place for a couple of years now, but Moore still found it hard to believe it had reached this stage with Ivory and Daggett. He pushed his horse hard into the brush, hoping to blot it out, temporarily, at least, with the sheer physical effort.

Ramadero was a border Mexican name for thicket, and some of these *ramaderos* covered many square miles, made up of smaller thickets, interlaced with game trails and open patches. There was a section four miles north of the house that had never been worked to Moore's knowledge, and, when he reached the fringe of this great *ramadero,* he tied his two neck oxen to a coma tree, and started threading his way into the dry jungle.

Within a few feet it got so thick he could hardly make

headway. He worked his horse painfully through a wall of mesquite and found a dim trail. Fifty feet down this he flushed a wild heifer. She rose with a great, crackling explosion from where she had crouched in a patch of mesquite.

"Let's go!" shouted Moore, and Hokey Pokey took off without benefit of gut hooks. He was a quarter animal, with a big rump that gave him a jack-rabbit getaway and short driving legs that set him close to the ground. The heifer galloped down the narrow trail to where it ended in a wall of black chaparral, and crashed right through this. Moore followed, ducking under the branch of a post oak that grew beyond. There was a heavy growth of agrito beyond that. These cattle had uncanny judgment of whether a thicket was penetrable or not, and this one veered sharply about the agrito. But Hokey Pokey had developed that same sense through the years of brush popping, and he threw himself head-on into the agrito. With his infinite faith in the animal, Moore hunched forward, eyes wide open, making no effort to rein Hokey Pokey around the thicket.

They plowed into the spiny agrito with a sickening rake of thorns across leather and hide. But Hokey Pokey had somehow spotted a patch open beyond, catching the heifer as it came around from skirting the edge of the agrito. Moore dabbed his rope on her. Hokey Pokey made ramrods of his forelegs, and the man was off him before the ground had quit trembling from the heifer's fall. After hog-tying the beef with short lengths of rawhide rope called *peales,* Moore left her there and went back for one of the neck oxen. Yoked to a tame ox, wild cattle could fight all they wanted, but sooner or later the tame animal would return to the home spread with the wild one in tow, worn and docile from his hopeless battle. When Moore reached the yoke animals, there was a bloody man sprawled on the ground beside them.

"Frío," he snapped, jumping off his animal.

"Ay," groaned Ivory Lamar's father, when Moore had turned him over. "I find these cattle I know somebody's on the roundup. How in hell you ever get into these *ramadero*. Nobody ever crazy enough to work him before."

"Maybe they didn't have a good enough horse," Moore told him. "Hokey Pokey'll find a way through a brick wall. What happened here? It's in the belly?"

"Sort of through the side meat," groaned Frío. "Somebody dry-gulch me over in Double Fork pastures, hah?"

Moore could not help saying it: "Maybe Warren don't like his cows butchered, either."

"Butchered? He-he." It was like an old squaw's giggle, and it brought a wince of pain from the gross Mexican. It was hard to reconcile Ivory's beauty to the prodigious ugliness of her father. The seams were burst on his *chivarras* by the beefy muscles of his thighs, and, although his gut made an immense pot before him, his hams were as lean as an alley cat's from a lifetime in the saddle. He had a thick mane of coarse, white hair and longhorn mustaches that flickered at his chest with each movement of his head. The pouches almost hiding his eyes were filled with the purple tracery of minute, broken veins that substantiated the tale of riotous, debauched living told by his great *retroussé* bulb of a nose. Evidently he had crawled this far on his hands and knees, from the signs he had left through the mesquite grass in the direction of the Double Fork.

Moore got Frío Lamar back to the Bootjack with great difficulty. Here he washed the wound and then got half a jug full of mescal. This brought a groan from Lamar.

"I always did think mescal made better disinfectant than liquor." Moore grinned. "Now I'm going to make you a poultice my grandmother taught me. It'll draw like a sulking bull, trying to pull loose of a coma tree. Just grind some charred oak bark with this Indian meal and mix it with tallow. There won't be any infection with that on you."

The man squinted up at him out of suspicious little eyes. "Why do you do this for me? Ivory say you shoot me on sight the next time."

"I will, if I catch you butchering my beef again." Moore shrugged.

"Ha-ha!" It was like the raucous bray of a mule this time, with Lamar throwing his shaggy head back. "You got too much vinegar for honest man." He turned his head aside in a strange, puckish gesture that left him looking obliquely up at Moore from under those shaggy brows. "You like my liddle girl, hah?"

"You know how I feel, Frío," said Moore.

"Is too bad Ivory don't appreciate such good hard-working man as you."

Moore was peeling the bark off some lengths of live oak he'd brought in to burn, and piling this in the coals of his fire to char for the poultice. "Maybe it's the way she's been brought up."

Frío's eyebrows raised in acknowledgment. "I don't deny. Not very good example, am I? She shouldn't have come home from that convent."

"I never thought you'd apologize for the way you lived."

"I'm not apologize," erupted Lamar. This effort brought a groan of pain from him, and he sank back. *"Ruego por mi alma . . . pray for my soul . . . that she hurt like diablo. "* He sighed, speaking quietly with effort. "I don't regret a thing I done, in all my life, not one liddle thing. I live good. I enjoy every minute. It's not question of work, lazy, or steal, or whatever you are. It's question of my girl being happy. You can't blame her for her ideas. My wife, she work like devil and die for it. Me, fat and happy, and strongest man in the brush at fifty, and never do a day's work in my life. Now tell me which is right. Ivory see Daggett go in town and pull down two, three hundred dollar one night on monte. Then you go work Double Fork five years for thirty a month and dump it all in a spread like this that give you nothing but grief."

"You'd think Ivory was the type to look a little deeper than that," sighed Moore.

"Maybe she could, if Daggett's glitter don't blind her so."

"You don't like Daggett?" asked Moore.

Lamar's fat shrug obliterated his ears. "He's *bueno* for monte game, maybe, or drink mescal with." His voice lashed out savagely. "But not for my liddle girl. . . ."

Again he had to settle back, breathing heavily with the pain of his wound. Moore had the bark charred and ground into Indian meal, and was heating the tallow in a tin can when the sound of crashing brush outside took him to the door. It was Ivory Lamar, fighting an excited, lathered horse into the clearing. The sight of her held palpable, poignant shock. She was wearing a man's blue denim shirt that did not fit her like it would a man, and her grease-slick *chivarras* were too tight across the hips for his comfort. She was bareheaded, her black hair in a tumbled, rendered mass down to her shoulders, full of burrs and thorns.

"Nolan," she said, "have you seen Dad? Something's happened to him. He went out last night and didn't come back. Kynette was over to our place this morning. He says there was a shooting on the Double Fork. He's got a warrant sworn out for Dad by Warren."

"Your father's inside," he said. "If Kynette hit your place, isn't he liable to come by here?"

She dropped down off her animal without answering, letting the reins ground-hitch it, and brushed by Moore with all her soft, fulsome weight striking him momentarily. It left him a little giddy. She was on her knees beside Frío when Moore gained the back room. She had not spoken before they heard the brush start popping again, away out.

"Get him out the back way," he hissed at her. "Hokey Pokey's in the pen, still saddled."

He helped her get Frío to the door, then wheeled and ran through the house to get Ivory's animal out of sight. He had just caught the reins up when three riders broke from the brush. Sheriff Kynette was in the lead, forking a horse with a lot of Arab in its slender legs and short back, as small and compact and lethal as the man himself.

The sheriff swung down with a typical economy of motion. He was even shorter than Moore, with a sense of catty balance to his square body. There were hard, weathered ridges at either side of his lips that came from a habitually compressed mouth, and his eyes gave the impression that more than the continual squinting in a hot country rendered them so eternally slitted.

"I'm after Frío Lamar, Moore," he said. "Can I take a look inside?"

"Without a warrant?"

"Don't make things tough." Kynette glanced at the animal Ivory had ridden. "You had a hard ride?"

"Just got back from roundup," said Moore.

"What happened to Hokey Pokey?"

"Man needs more than one animal for a string, Sheriff."

As Kynette pushed past Moore with a faint grimace and went toward the house, Gerry Warren bent out of the saddle. He was the owner of the Double Fork, a tall, spare man in scarred broadcloth trousers and town-coat, his white collar open and wilted with sweat.

"I'm sorry about this, Nolan. Take it easy on Kynette. You know how he gets when he's on a trail."

"Come in here, Moore!" called the sheriff, from the house. Moore dropped the reins and walked through the front door. Kynette was standing in the bedroom. "What is this on these blankets? Dried blood?"

"I spilled some wine."

"What's your bed doing all messed up if you were on roundup?"

"A man gets careless batching it."

"It's still warm."

"Been a hot day."

III

Kynette stalked back into the front room, pinning Moore with eyes cold and unwinking as the business ends of two guns. "I always wondered why a hand as smart as you would mortgage himself up to the neck in a jinx outfit like this. The only answer I could ever get was that you'd figured some way to beat the rustling before you moved in. What kind of an arrangement do you have with them, Moore?"

"No arrangement except what I pack in my holster," said Moore.

"Don't feed me that hay. Everybody knows how thick you've been with the Lamars these last years."

"Is Lamar a rustler?" asked Moore.

"He was shot on my Double Fork last night by my foreman," said Warren, from the doorway.

Moore turned to see that Kynette's deputy was following Warren in, a heavy-shouldered, black-headed young man with his eyes on Moore but enough attention on Kynette to take directions. "Maybe he was butchering a beef," Moore said. "I've had the same trouble with my stuff."

"Most brush poppers only butcher one animal at a time when they're out after meat," said Warren. "He had a dozen in the cut he was running toward the river. My foreman tried to find him after shooting him off his horse, but Frío crawled off into the thickets."

"Moore's bed's been slept in today and there's blood on the blanket, Gerry," Kynette told the Double Fork owner. "Are you satisfied?"

Moore saw the subtle alteration of Warren's gaunt face. The passive reluctance left and was replaced by a growing anger that drew enough blood in his cheeks to darken them perceptibly as he turned on Moore.

"Nolan, if you're hiding something, you'd better tell us. I'm up against the wall with this rustling. I'd hate to think you were mixed up with it. Give us some help, won't you? We'll give you the benefit of the doubt. If you know where Frío Lamar is, tell us."

"I'll give you as much help as Kynette gave me when I was having trouble," said Moore.

Kynette's boots made a small, scraping sound against the hard earthen floor. "You shouldn't have said that, Moore."

"You'll have to excuse me," said Moore. "Us little operators don't swing as big a loop as the Double Fork come election time, do we, Kynette?"

Kynette's pinched nostrils fluttered. "Are you going to tell us where Frío is?"

"To be perfectly honest, I don't know."

"Put him in that chair, Stone."

Moore whirled toward the deputy, realizing the mistake of letting them come in behind him that way, through the door. But the man must have been half waiting for something like that. He was already moving, fast and hard, and his young, beefy weight bulled Moore back into the wall before Moore could set himself. Then his knee rose against Moore's crotch. The utter lack of personal feeling made its force all the more vicious. Moore doubled over, almost vomiting with the pain. Stone caught him under the armpits and spun him over into a chair.

"Kynette!" said Warren.

"Let me handle it, Gerry," said Kynette.

Moore tried to stop Stone from throwing the rope around him, but his reactions were dead, and with that nauseating agony in his groin he had no will. They lashed him into the rawhide-seated chair, and then Kynette stood directly before him, the ridges at the corners of his lips deepened with their further compression.

"Now listen, Moore. You know what a thankless job it is for an officer in a county like Webb. Every other man out in this brush has gotten a few cows wet in his time. Sooner or later, we pick up those pot-rack operators. That's like trying to kill a rat-tail cactus by cutting off one thorn at a time. There's a center to this thing, one bunch that we've never been able to nail, one bunch that's been running the majority of the cattle across the river through the years. We know they pull in so much beef they couldn't possibly get rid of it all right away. They've got to have some place out in the brush where they hold it till they find a market."

"I've got a big pen out back," said Moore, shaking his head. "It'll hold at least two dozen cows."

Kynette stepped in and slapped him across the face so hard it knocked his head back. "I'll beat enough of the salt out of you to give me a straight answer if it takes all day," said the sheriff in a thin, restrained whisper. "Now you know where they hold the cattle, and you know where Frío has gone. I think they're both at the same place. Let's have it."

"I don't know, Kynette."

Kynette's slap jerked his head to one side. "That's a lie!"

Senses singing, Moore did not answer. There was a wonder in him at why he was doing this. He owed Lamar nothing. He had no illusions about the old reprobate. If Lamar was in with that gang, he deserved to be turned in. Moore would have turned him in the day before, eagerly. Yet, now he remembered how instinctively he had seen to their escape, without considering the consequences, or asking himself whether Lamar was a rustler. And he knew why. Ivory. It came to him like that, in a sudden flash. If they caught Frío, it would implicate her.

"Come on, Moore!" Kynette struck him with a fist this time. "Is it Red Thickets?"

"I dunno. . . ."

"Dagger Island?"

"Now you're getting foolish, Kynette," he snapped. "You couldn't get a boat on Dagger Island, much less a cow."

"It's got to be somewhere. Come on, Moore." Kynette hit him again. "Is it Little River?" That dull explosion of knuckles again. "The Swamp?"

"I dunno, I tell you, I dunno. . . ."

In a spasm he could not control, Moore tried to tear loose of the bonds. His struggles upset the chair and his head struck hard earth with a stunning impact. Dimly he felt them lifting him up again, chair and all. Kynette came back to it. Each blow held calculated viciousness, yet was as dispassionate as ice.

"Kynette, stop it!"

"Let me alone, Warren. This is my hand." Leering down at Moore: "Ramaderos Blancas?" Slugging him. "Where is it, where is it?"

Moore lost measure of time. The whole room expanded and contracted. He could not breathe. He had too much breath. His mouth filled with blood. He passed out once, and they revived him with a bucket of water. After an interminable period of battering torture, there were no more blows. There was the sound of their voices, discussing something. Then Stone was untying the rope and letting Moore slump from the chair to the floor. After another giddy space, Moore heard the sound of horses outside. He tried to get on his feet and could not.

He crawled around the room, hunting what was left of that mescal he'd used on Lamar. He found the jug smashed in a corner. When he heard sound at the door, he thought it was Kynette again and stifled a bitter, defeated groan with effort. Then Ivory's face was before him, and he noticed in some wry, dim corner of his attention that the room was almost dark. Had it been that long?

"Oh, you fool, you fool," she kept saying over and over. She got some water at the creek and doused him in this and used the remainder to make a bitter, black pot of coffee. He sat slumped over at the table, struggling with nausea.

"Where's Frío?" he asked finally, apathetically.

"He fell off Hokey Pokey out in the brush and I couldn't get him back on alone." She had to force the coffee down Moore. "You think you can get enough strength to help me with him? He isn't fit to travel, Nolan. Even to our spread."

"I don't think they'll be back here for a while. I think I convinced Kynette I didn't know anything."

She straightened above him, a strange, indefinable expression filling her face. "Do you know what they did to your cattle?"

He let the realization seep slowly into his dulled mind, with his knowledge of Kynette, and then his bruised, bloody face took on a bleak, empty look. "I guess so. I haven't got any left?"

"Or pens, either. They did a very thorough job of it. They wrecked all three of your pens and turned the beef into the brush again." She came and put her hands on the table, staring in a twisted effort to comprehend something. "Why did you do it? Why didn't you tell them? You knew what Kynette was capable of, if you bucked him."

He saw now what she could not reconcile. "Wouldn't you have done it, in my place?" he asked softly. She frowned, without answer. He took a sip of coffee, staring at the wall. "Or should I say, wouldn't Daggett have done it?"

Her head tossed defiantly. "All right. Maybe he wouldn't. Does that make you the little tin saint?"

"Ivory, you don't mean that. Frío's your father."

"I do mean it. I'd mean it if you'd done it for me, or anybody else. You were ready to shoot Dad the other day. Lee may not be a saint, but at least he's consistent."

Moore rose shakily, reaching for her elbow. "Ivory, what do you really feel for Daggett?"

The planes of her face were hard, unyielding. "What do you think?"

"Frío said his glitter blinded you," Moore told her. "I had a horse once like that. So beautiful everybody wanted him. But he didn't have any bottom when it came to the grind."

"And you have, is that it?"

"I'm not making comparisons. You just got to see what Daggett really is."

"You *are* making comparisons! You can't help it." Her voice fanned him like a flame. "What *is* Lee? Just because he's smart enough to make his living without work. What are you, for that matter? You put so much faith in this bottom when it comes to the grind. It's a grind, all right. Eighteen hours a day out in those thickets and what does it get you? You're so careful to follow a straight trail all your life and work yourself to death and then someone on your side of the river comes along and beats you up for it and smashes what you've been building for months. I'll take Lee Daggett any day."

"You can't!"

The vehemence of his voice surprised even him, and stiffened Ivory, her green eyes narrowing at him. "Why can't I?" she said in a soft, speculative tone.

Even in his weakened condition, the nearness of her filled him with a powerful urge he could not deny. "Is this a good enough reason?" he said, moving himself in against her. Her whole body surged upward against him with the kiss. At first, he thought she would fight it. She didn't.

When he finally drew his lips away, her eyes were closed, and her deep bosom was rising and falling tautly against the denim shirt. He found it difficult to speak.

"Maybe I should have said it that way first, without all this talk. You've known how I felt, Ivory. For a long time. You know what it did to me when I came on you and Daggett kissing that way. I would have spoken before, but I had so little to offer when I was working for Warren. I wanted to wait till I got hold of something like this and developed it into a decent security for a woman. A thirty-and-found hand hasn't even got the right to speak like this. But a man with his own outfit. . . ."

She shook her head, eyes still closed, as if not wanting to look at him. "It's too late. I'm sorry. Whatever you feel, I'm sorry."

"You feel it, too, Ivory. It's in your face now. Why do you try to hide it?"

"No," she almost cried, shaking her head violently from side to side, eyes pinched shut. "Come on. We've got to get

Dad. It's too late, I tell you."

He grabbed her elbows fiercely. "Why is it too late?"

Her eyes opened at last, with the defiant backward toss of her head. "Lee Daggett and I were married in Laredo last night."

IV

It took Frío Lamar a long time to heal, back in that fetid little room. Moore nursed him through a succession of days that had lost meaning. He had not thought himself capable of feeling such a great emotional shock. In a numb haze he had helped Ivory get her father back to the house. Frío had worn himself out, raging about the marriage. There had been a last, bitter scene between father and daughter, and she had left, riding off into the night.

About the fourth day, Frío was able to sit up and eat. After finishing an enormous meal, he belched monstrously, and spat on the floor.

"This is the foulest mess of hog tripe I ever taste!"

Moore sighed heavily. "It is?"

"He-he," giggled Frío, looking up in that sly, sideways glance. "You really lost the old salt, don't you? Week ago you would have shamed me into silence with your comebacks. Now all you do is sigh, and ask me, is it? *¡Valgame!* You know it isn't. Good food. Good man. Good, honest man, with more guts and vinegar than any honest man deserves. So she goes and marries that yellow-haired *lépero*."

Moore's head came up as he realized what Lamar had been driving at. He could not help but grin wanly. He realized he was forming an attachment for the old reprobate. Whatever Frío really was, he held a rich, animal talent for living, a naïve, childish simplicity that drew Moore.

"Trouble is, Daggett's so handsome, such big lover. Same way as me when I'm young. Maybe not as big lover. But same way. You can't tell girls about that. They got to learn themselves. Got to get hurt. Now she get hurt." Frío spat disgustedly. "What happen here didn't help matters any. You can see how it looks to Ivory. It don't help your argument for that straight trail and hard work much, when the very men you ride it with come along and beat you up for it. ¡Caracoles!" He giggled with great care to keep from hurting his stomach, glancing slyly at Moore. "Why you take that beating, hah?"

"I couldn't see Kynette picking up a man in your condition. He was just as liable to have given it to you the same way."

"It wasn't for me that much." Frío measured what Moore had done with a greasy thumb and forefinger. "Maybe liddle bit for me. I like to think that. But mainly for Ivory, hah?" He studied Moore for a moment, then spoke again, in a different tone. "Got to be a lot of gravel in the craw for take a beating like that, Moore." He paused again, and the speculation was plain in his twinkling eyes now. "I always wonder, Moore, just what you planned to do if you ever did snag onto the men who was rustle your beef. You must have some idea in mind."

"I'd feed them to the buzzards," said Moore through tight lips.

"Por Dios, you are all alone," Frío told him. "There must be a gang of them. You wouldn't just walk up to them like you came over to my place and ask them to stop taking your beef."

"I'd do whatever was necessary to stop them."

Frío bent closer, peering at him in a puzzled, slightly mocking way. "No. I cannot believe. Even you are not that salty. Just walk into their camp all alone, and. . . ."

"Just give me a chance."

That great belly began to quiver. Moore waited till the chuckle spread upward, pouting out the fat lips. Frío lay back and let it roll forth in great chortling bubbles.

"I like to see that. I really like to see that," he laughed. It took a long time to subside. When he spoke again, he was still lying back, grinning at the ceiling. "You ever heard of Dos Águilas?"

"Two Eagles?" Moore shrugged. "I was there once. Ten miles below the border."

"*Sí.* It is said lot of cattle are sold there. A man named Ardiente Martínez is suppose to be especially active in the business."

Moore found himself inclined toward the man, a strange, tingling sensation filling him. "What are you driving at?"

"Why don't you go there and find out?"

Dos Águilas was no different than a thousand other border towns on either side of the Río Grande. The adobe houses clustered like dusty cubes around the main plaza, scattering themselves outward from this square along twisting, narrow lanes fruity with the redolence of fresh onions and stale leather and ancient mud. Nolan Moore came into the plaza via one of these lanes near nightfall, about a week after Kynette had visited the Bootjack.

Frío Lamar was still staying at the Bootjack, but he could care for himself now. Moore had no idea why the old scoundrel should drop this kind of a lead, but he meant to follow it for all he was worth. If it meant Frío did not belong to the rustlers, he was glad. If the man were putting him into some kind of a trap, he did not care; he welcomed a meeting with the rustlers under any circumstances.

Moore had a drink at one of the *cantinas* and dropped word he was looking for cattle. Then he took a room at the inn on the plaza. He moved the tin sconce so the candle would not backlight him, when he opened the door, and then sat down to wait. In about half an hour, the knock came. He pulled the door partway open, to reveal two men.

One was tall and slim and immaculately tailored in a black fustian and moleskin trousers. His face was smooth, and his lips held a vulpine facility, slithering into a smile. The candlelight made little pinpoints of glittering light in the restless movement of his eyes as they took in the room behind Moore.

"Ardiente Martínez is my name," he said. "This is Sliver."

Sliver was shorter than Ardiente Martínez. Moore had seen many men with scarred faces. He had never seen one like this. The history of the knife itself seemed to have been carved into it. One of the ears was literally hacked to fringe, the other missing completely. A groove slashed through the twisted nose and looked like an axe had been at work. One eye was closed by a nauseous ridge of peeling, purple scar tissue. The other was squinted shut above a cheek that had been flayed open, leaving a livid patch of healed flesh, pink and smooth and ghastly. There were a myriad of others, splitting his lips and cleaving his chin.

"Do not lose such a good supper, *señor*," smiled Martínez, seeing the expression on Moore's face. "You will get used to Sliver in a while. He is just overly fond of the knife, and cannot help reflecting it in his . . . shall we say . . . face." The laugh trickled out like oil. "I understand you are interested in cattle."

"Not at Kansas prices," said Moore, stepping back.

Martínez moved in, rubbing his hands together, grinning slyly. "I am not speaking for myself, you understand, but I have a friend who is in temporary financial distress. He has a few cows he might like to sell. You would have to overlook a few things, of course."

"How about two-fifty a head?"

Martínez held up his hands in shock. "Oh, *señor*, you insult the very cows themselves. Six dollars a head or nothing."

"Give you four-and-a-half if I can have a look at them first."

"We'll settle for five, payment on delivery."

Moore shook his head. "I don't mind a few of them getting wet in the river. But I do want decent beef."

Martínez shook his head. "This friend of mine is sort of touchy. He would not like that kind of a deal. I give you my word the beef is good. If you will give me half the money now, I will have the beef here tomorrow night."

Moore shook his head. "No look, no deal."

The horribly scarred man touched the hilt of a Bowie stuck in his belt. "How stubborn. Perhaps he would like my sliver under his fingernail."

"Don't be impetuous," Martínez said. "Please, *señor*, you are being unreasonable. You must know the considerations in an affair like this. My friend does not want to meet any more people than necessary."

"Where's he holding the cattle?" asked Moore.

"Now he is getting inquisitive," said Sliver, winding the fingers of his hand around the hilt of that knife. Moore knew the foolishness of waiting for this kind to make the first move. He had been waiting for them to make the moves too long now. His vicious forward lunge took Sliver by surprise. The man tried to leap back, but Moore put a charging shoulder into his chest and grabbed the knife wrist with both hands. It carried Sliver back against the door with a crash that brought a grunt of pain from him.

By the time they had reached this position, Moore had that wrist twisted around far enough to force Sliver to drop the Bowie. From the tail of his eye, he saw that Martínez had jumped back, but had made no move to pull anything. Moore brought his boot in a vicious scuffing kick against Sliver's ankles. It upset the man, and Moore dumped him in the corner with a helping shove against his shoulder.

"You stay right there till we finish our business," Moore told him in a flat, casual voice, and turned to Martínez. "I'm glad you leave the dirty work to your pig-sticker. You'll find it easier to talk without lumps on your head. How about telling me where those cattle are?"

The man knitted his eyebrows in anguish. "Why are you Texans always this way?"

The brush south of the river wasn't much different than that on the other side. Martínez and Sliver had horses outside the inn, and, after getting his animal from the hostler, Moore allowed them to ride ahead of him out into the thickets. The mesquite trees were black-barked ghouls in the dusk, their branches weeping like a willow's under the hoary weight of mistletoe gathered through the years. The unharvested beans of countless past springs lay thick and crackling underfoot, all the way to the Río Grande. The tide was turning saffron under a rising moon, and they rode upriver till an island blocked their view to the other shore. The sharp blades of the yuccas covering this island thrust against the sky like a thousand daggers. Martínez turned his horse down a crumbling bank.

"This can't be it," Moore told him. "Even the Indians can't make it over there."

"I'm glad you agree," said Martínez. "Now, if you will just leave things up to me, I will bring you the cattle tomor—"

"Get on with it," interrupted Moore flatly.

"Santa María," murmured the man. He took out a match, cupped it against the wind, then turned the opening of his

hand three times toward the island. In a moment, Moore saw an answering trio of yellow pinpoints flashing on and off. Martínez put his horse along the bank, bending out of the saddle till he seemed to find some sort of landmark, and then put his horse into the shallows. Moore let Sliver precede him, then followed with Hokey Pokey, deliberately relaxing his body so the horse would not feel his nervousness. It was still hard to accept this.

Even the Indians had no traditions of ever gaining Dagger Island. The channel was so deep here that there was no known ford within ten miles on either side, and any boats attempting to land on the island were swept past it by an irresistible current.

Moore could feel Hokey Pokey's barrel shudder with the heavy, beating sweep of water against it. The horse laid his ears back and started tossing his head violently. Moore spoke quietly to him all the rest of the way, patting him against a wet neck. There seemed to be some sort of ridge they walked on. More than once the animal was swept downstream, wetting Moore to the waist before he fought back up onto the high sand.

As they approached the island, the current became stronger. Martínez and Sliver turned their animals head-on into it, facing upriver, and they finished the walk sidestepping like a bunch of circus horses. They reached the bank soaked to the skin, the horses worn out by the nervous tension and the heavy battle with the current.

"What is it?" Moore asked. "A sandbar?"

"It is there from about April to September," said Martínez. "The spring floods form it, and it doesn't wash away completely till the end of summer. And this is Blackeye."

The man materialized out of the darkness like a tall,

stooped wraith. Greasy jeans hung on bony legs by one gallus, and his cotton shirt was in shreds from riding the brush. He had an ugly, horsy face with a black patch over one eye.

"This is a buyer, Blackeye," Martínez told him.

The good eye glittered. "You know better'n to bring him here."

"He insisted," said Martínez.

"What've you got Sliver for?" asked Blackeye.

"I'm beginning to wonder," Martínez sighed.

This brought a shrill peal of laughter from Blackeye. There was a wild howling note to it that touched some primeval chord in Moore, raising the hairs down the back of his neck.

"You mean he blotted Sliver's brand?" asked the man.

"And dumped him in the corner like a sack of meal," said Martínez.

"That's as good as an engraved invitation where I'm concerned, stranger." Blackeye grinned at Moore. "I ain't never seen Sliver handled like that before."

"Too much talk makes me nervous," said Moore. "Let's take a look at things."

Blackeye cast a last, wild, laughing glance at him and turned to get a brush-scarred old buckskin out of some mesquite. They followed a well-beaten trail through thick brush, over a chain of low hills and into a valley full of bawling, nervous cattle. Moore saw half a dozen different earmarks in the herd. He caught the Double Fork's swallowtail, and his own seven under-bit more than once. Then they topped more hills and rode into a small box cañon with the yellow squares of lighted windows at the end. They dismounted, Blackeye calling something into the first building. There was an answer, and the opening door splashed its yellow illumination

113

outward. Moore let Martínez and Sliver precede him. He tried to go after Blackeye, but the grinning man insisted on being last.

It was the usual low-roofed adobe, with round cottonwood *viga* poles for rafters, a bull's-eye lantern suspended from one of these above a rickety plank table. The first one Moore placed was Lee Daggett. Lantern light glimmered across the greasy sheath of his tight leather leggings and jacket, made a bright, sharp flash on his depthless eyes as he recognized Moore.

"Where in the hell did you pick him up?" he said in a sharp loud voice.

Moore had already taken that swift, sliding step aside, to place his back against the wall by the door, bringing Blackeye into the scope of his attention, as well as all others in the room.

"He forced me, Lee," said Martínez defensively. "You should see what he did to Sliver. I'm getting a new man."

"One more chance, Ardiente," muttered Sliver. "I'll give you his whole hide in one strip. You can make a twenty-foot bullwhip out of it."

"You're a damn' fool, Moore," said Daggett.

Moore's grin held no humor. "I'll remember everything you say, Daggett. I must admit this is some surprise to me. This kind of work is so dirty. I could never quite see you soiling your hands on cattle . . . even wet cattle."

Daggett's body seemed to lift itself upward. Moore felt the tension of the whole room press him against the wall like a physical weight. Then it was Ivory, moving slowly from a short hallway that led to the back rooms, staring in a twisted disbelief at Moore. That old poignancy struck him, with his first sight of her. But there was something else. He could not define it at first. She was dressed in a flowered calico dress he had seen on her before. There were smudges down one side of it, and her red Spanish shoes were scuffed and dirty. There was something in her eyes, too. At first, he had seen the flashing light fill them with surprised anger. But that was gone, leaving something almost furtive.

"What do you want here, Nolan?" she said in a husky tone.

"First I'd like the name of that man standing to your right, Ivory," said Moore.

"What for?" The nervous, incisive edge to Daggett's voice made sharp contrast to Ivory's diffused tone.

"He's the only one I haven't been introduced to yet, and I'd like to know who I'm whipping if I ever run across him picking up my cattle again," said Moore.

That wild, pealing laughter of Blackeye's filled the room again, as he threw back his shaggy head. "This 'poke really cuts his biscuits, Daggett."

"Shut up, Blackeye," said Daggett irritably.

"Why?" grinned the man. "I think you ought to introduce him. The man you inquire for is Paint, stranger. He claims he was burnt in a fire once, but he really skinned that hide off the rump of his pinto horse and got it stuck in his face while it was still wet."

"You're going to make that joke once too often, Blackeye," said Paint sullenly. He was a slop-gutted, bow-legged man about Moore's height, his face and hands covered with great brownish patches of skin.

"I won't say I'm glad to make your acquaintance, Paint," said Moore. "You and Daggett and Blackeye will do. We might as well start now."

"Start what?" said Daggett.

"Why, cutting out the Bootjack cows you have in that herd and driving them back to my spread," said Moore.

This time Blackeye did not laugh. He stared at Moore with

his gaunt, equine face twisted in some effort of comprehension. Daggett's face filled slowly with blood, till it seemed to glow under the lantern light. Then an inarticulate curse left him, and all his weight surged forward onto his toes, when Moore's voice stopped him.

"You wouldn't do it with a woman in the room, would you?"

Daggett was leaning so far forward he actually swayed. The white stag butts of his twin Forehands swayed with him. His elbows were hooked backward, the tips of his fingers pointed at the handle of each gun in plain advertisement of his intent. He remained that way a moment, a dozen shades of emotion passing through his face. All the other men were watching him with a painful intensity, like dogs waiting for some word from their master. Finally, with a faint twitch of his scored lips, he took three deliberate steps toward the wall. Ivory still stood at the door, a dozen feet behind him, but she would now be directly in the line of fire, if Moore shot at Daggett.

"I'm glad you reminded me of that, Moore," grinned Daggett. "I'm giving you one more chance to leave."

The consideration clicked through Moore's mind in swift succession during that last moment. A man with a gun usually had an edge on a knife artist when it came to unlimbering the weapon, and Martínez had already shown his colors when it came to action. Both Sliver and Martínez were on Moore's right, near the front wall. He could leave them till the last. Only Daggett and Paint were in front of him. Between them, the first to consider was Daggett. Unable to shoot the man for fear of hitting Ivory, Moore would have to block him out some way. And he had the way. Blackeye stood to Moore's left, about an arm's length away.

"I'll leave the three of you and my cattle," said Moore, the mild, casual tone of his voice leaving them so unprepared for what followed that he had an edge on every man in the room. He lashed out to hook one hand in Blackeye's waistband, grab the man's shoulder in the other, and spin him around bodily toward Daggett. Off balance, Blackeye could not help stumbling backward under Moore's heave, crashing into Daggett before the man had his guns free, and carrying him back against the wall with such force that they both fell to the floor.

As soon as he had released Blackeye, Moore went for his gun. He put a bullet through Paint's leg before the man had his own iron skinned, and saw him pitch forward onto his face. Before Paint had hit, Moore had his gun switched toward the other way. Sliver had that Bowie pulled back of his ear for a throw, and it stayed there. Moore had pegged Martínez right, too. The man stood against the wall, startled and pacific, staring in owlish admiration at the carnage.

"You really clean the plate off, don't you, *señor?*" he said.

"I've had this kind of grub before," Moore informed him. "Now, if you'll help Blackeye get up off Daggett, we'll do the little job of work I mentioned before."

V

The cavalcade reached Bootjack near the hottest part of the next day. It had been a sweating, maddening, devilish job to drive that big a bunch of wild cattle back across the river and through the thick brush on the north side. Moore had to forget the ones that got away, because he was afraid the men he let out to capture them would simply not come back.

As it was, they came into the Bootjack clearing with a dozen head, Moore bringing up the rear with his gun out, a grim, gaunt figure, sweat making white streaks through the grimed flesh of his face, his eyes red-rimmed and feverish from lack of sleep. At the door of the house, waiting for them beneath the arbor, was that great, kettle-bellied man with the leonine mane of white hair. Moore could see that great belly quivering from clear across the clearing. Frío had his hands spread out across it as if to hold something in, his head thrown backward as he laughed.

"*Valgame Dios,* no, I cannot believe it. He didn't do it. All of you together, like rounding up the beef. *Qué barbaridad.* I never thought I'd see the day. Moore, I can't believe it. Did you really make Martínez take you to the island? Sliver and all?"

Daggett climbed down off Smoke, staring tightly at Frío. "How did you know?"

Frío was still chuckling when he turned toward Daggett, but the tone had changed. "*Dios,* now, how do you suppose? Maybe the brush rustle in some wind."

"You been here all the time?" said Daggett. He squinted his eyes, looking at Frío. "You didn't tell him?"

"Now, why should I do that?" Frío's body had stopped quivering; he had only a grin now.

"You told him about Martínez?" Daggett's voice had risen to a shrill, sharp edge. "You sent him in there . . . !"

"Any man with the sand enough to walk in and take over the whole bunch of you deserves to be told," said Frío. "Did you ever see such a *hombre,* Daggett? More sand than a riverbank."

"So you tell him everything," said Daggett. "We've been working a month to get a nice big herd of stuff together, and then just because you take a liking to some greasy-sack brush popper, you send him in to bust it all up."

Frío's head turned aside from the man so that he was

looking at Daggett from the tail of his eyes in that sly, puckish, oblique way, a nasty twist to his smile now. "Can you think of any better reason, Daggett?"

"I can think of a more logical one," said Daggett. His voice sounded strained, as if forcing this out. "Maybe it had to do with Moore's sand, all right. But maybe you hoped that sand would extend to a little gun play."

"Daggett." Frío's shaggy brows lifted in puckish protest. "How you speak."

"Well, it did," said Daggett. "Moore shot Paint in the leg, and we had to leave him on the island. Does that disappoint you, Frío? Were you hoping it would be me, instead? More than just my leg, maybe?"

"You have such odd idea, Daggett," said Frío. "A man must be pretty unease in his mind when he starts for suspect his own father-in-law of such sad things. What makes you so unease? You shouldn't be, you know. It was the Double Fork foreman who shot me that night. Everybody think that. It wasn't one of my own bunch try for dry-gulch me."

The light caught Daggett's eyes just right, as he leaned toward Frío. They glittered, blank as panes of glass. "What did you say?" he asked, each word a chunk of lead dropped deliberately into the pool of silence.

"How did it feel for to be boss?" There was nothing left of that sly, puckish naïveté in Frío's eyes now, looking directly at Daggett. "You always like the idea of rodding a crew, didn't you, Daggett?"

"You ain't saying . . . ?"

"I ain't saying nothing." It left Frío in a roar. "I'm tired of saying. You ain't boss any more, Daggett. Frío Lamar's back, and he don't waste so much time in talk."

"You're wasting this time," said Daggett, and started to take a step that would put him within reach of Frío, lifting a vicious hand. But Ivory was off her horse, and she got in between them, pushing Daggett back.

"Let him alone, you fool. He's been wounded."

"That ain't the only reason he better leave me alone," growled Frío. In Ivory's struggle with Daggett, her head got twisted around till her glance crossed Moore, where he was still sitting on his horse, leaning forward against his crossed arms on the saddle horn, his right hand holding a gun pointed in Daggett's general direction. The others seemed to become aware of his presence then, utter silence only accentuating its domination. Frío stared at him, started to giggle, stopped with a wince of pain.

"This whole little show has been right interesting," said Moore. "So you've been the ramrod all along, Frío?"

"Who else could have made so much trouble for so many lawmen?"

"Why did you bother butchering my stuff for meat?"

Frío grinned. "If I didn't butcher anything, people wonder where I get my meat. So I butcher a steer now and then, like any other poor brush popper. *¿Es bueno?*"

"Pretty good," said Moore. "It sort of threw me off the trail."

"Now what you do?"

"I'd like your bunch to mend those corrals Kynette smashed so we'll have some place to hold these steers."

"Ha-haw. . . ." This time Frío could not contain the great, raucous eruption, pain and all. He roared and chuckled and chortled, swaying back and forth to slap his thigh. "What I tell you, *compadres?* More salt than El Paso. Did you ever see such a *hombre.* Funny part of it is, you get it done, Moore. You heard what he said, *hombres,* get to work on those pens."

"Now wait a minute, Frío," protested Martínez. "I'm not the man for that. You know how. . . ."

"I said get to work on those pens!" shouted Frío. "Do you want me to break your neck?"

They let Sliver circle-herd the cattle while the others mended the pens. Ivory went in to make coffee and beans for them from Moore's meager larder. After that she went over to the Lamar spread to get a horse for Frío. Everyone was sitting around inside, finishing the meal, when Frío came over to put his arm around Moore's shoulder, belching affectionately in his face.

"Maybe Daggett was right, in a way, *amigo*." He chuckled in a voice loud enough for them all to hear. "Frío's not big fool as he look, sometime. Maybe I have more reason for tell you about Martínez than just I like a man with guts. Maybe I like to see just how much guts you really got. I sure find out, hah? More guts than you can hang on a fence. We Mexicans have liddle different way of polishing off a horse than you. No matter how good he looks in corral, we don't pronounce him good cow horse till he's prove it on the range."

"You mean sort of a test," said Moore.

"That's right." Frío grinned. "And you came through good enough to ride any river with. There's never a man got the drop on my bunch that way before. We can't afford to have the man that did it on the outside. How about signing on my outfit? You could still have your ranch here. Sort of a front for us. Build it fast with the moneys you get from our business on the other side. Wouldn't even have to go in your own thickets for cattle. Blot a few brands here and there and you have a Bootjack herd to send north. You'd be bigger than Warren in a couple years. Big enough to see that Kynette gets what he deserves."

"Don't be a damn' fool, Frío," snarled Daggett.

"That's dangerous thing to call me, Daggett," said Frío.

The whispering tone of his voice was so irreconcilable with his usual roar that it held shocking threat.

"Never mind," Moore said. "It doesn't appeal to me."

"Oh, come on, Moore," pleaded Frío. "You got too much gravel in the craw for an honest man. You'd make the marvelous rustler. You and me together would drive Kynette crazy."

Moore shook his head. "I don't like it, Frío."

Frío sniffled in that habitual, childish way, giving an absent, sloppy swipe at his nose with a horny thumb. *"Caramba,"* he said with a sad shake of his head. "What a loss to the brotherhood." He took his arm off Moore's shoulders. "But that don't mean we ain't still *amigos.*"

"You leave my cows alone," said Moore.

"Is done." Frío chuckled. "Not another Bootjack cow will be touch. You hear that, *compadres?*" Frío wheeled to the men, beating himself on the chest. "From now on, anybody get a Bootjack cow wet, they answer to me. Not just you here. Anybody in the brush. Bootjack is sacred as a church from now on. That's the word of Frío Lamar!"

How strong a word that was, Moore found out in the days following. The bunch left that night, and Moore felt a strange, indefinable sadness fill him as he watched the gross, white-haired old man lead them off into the brush. He could not deny the attachment he had formed for Frío—rustler though he might be. He went back into the house and sat up half the night, with the old man on his mind—and Ivory. What bitter pain it had been to see her again, as Daggett's wife.

In the scant, grudging attention she had shown him, he had felt a new, insidious alteration in her that he could not quite define. The old fire had been there in the haughty defiance of what glances she did allow to meet his, but they had shifted away so quickly, almost furtively, as if there were some vague fear of looking at him too long. Finally Moore threw himself into the bunk.

The next morning a pair of brush poppers were squatted beneath his arbor when he came out. They were the two men he had taken in to Sheriff Kynette long ago on the butchering charge, typical of the strange, wild hermits of this bizarre country, bearded and taciturn, as scarred and leprous from the tearing brush as the wild cattle. They said they were willing to work for him and would take pay in meat or wait till he got the money from his trail herd. Moore saw Frío Lamar's hand in this and accepted their services without question.

Three days later another man joined him, appearing mysteriously out of the brush. With this growing crew, Moore soon had more beef than his pens could hold and was building new corrals. He contacted a big outfit in McMullen County and made arrangements to send his four-year-olds north with their trail herd. At prevailing prices, this would give him enough for his payment on the mortgage and leave quite a chunk over. For the first time since he had taken over the Bootjack, he was beginning to see his way clear. Then—it was two weeks to the day since Frío had left, with not one steer butchered and no signs of rustling—Moore brought his crew back to the spread late in the evening with a full quota of struggling, sulling wild ones, and found every one of his pens smashed, and every one of his cows gone.

None of the brush poppers would go with him, of course. The trail was easy to follow. He hoped to catch them before they reached the island. He rode in a black fit of rage, hardly able to think along more than that one line to find them. He knew dim surprise when the trail ended in a holding ground near Comanche Ford on this side.

There were several campfires with coals still warm, and

bloody bits of flesh left on the ground from cutting new ear-marks. That meant they had blotted his brand and earmark here instead of waiting till the island. The puzzle of it only added to the anger in him. Sign said they had gone into the ford after doing the redecorating, and he crossed after them, following the trail up to the sandbar. It was a rough crossing; he was almost swept away three or four times. Dripping wet, he gained the island, pushing Hokey Pokey inland.

The herd bawled restlessly in that pocket between the hills, without necessity of a rider. He threaded through them till he found what he wanted. It would pass pretty close in-spection later, but now the freshly cut earmarks had not yet healed. His seven under-bit had been obliterated by an under half-crop. His Bootjack brand had been changed to Lazy Skewbar. He went the rest of the way through darkness of night at a gallop.

They were all playing poker in the front room of the main shack when he burst through the door. Frío twisted around in his chair. Daggett half rose, starting to reach for a gun. Then he stopped, with sight of the Colt in Moore's hand.

"Moore, *compadre*." Frío grinned. "You come to join us after all, hah."

"I came to take the bunch of you in to Kynette," said Moore. "With the evidence so fresh you can still draw blood by squeezing those ears."

Frío's whole face seemed to collapse inward with an al-most ludicrous effort of comprehension. Then his face began to fill with blood, until its darkness was almost Negroid, and he turned back to Daggett.

"You didn't," he said in a barely audible voice.

Daggett stared sullenly at him, without answering.

"So that's why you changed the brands on the mainland

instead of waiting till here," said Frío. His voice was growing louder now. "I ought to kill you."

"Frío!" shouted Daggett, trying to jump up, but Frío had already heaved the table up and over on him. The others upset their chairs, trying to keep from getting tangled in the upsetting table, and Paint made a habitual stab for iron.

"You want another game leg?" Moore shouted at him, and it stopped the man. Frío had jumped over the upturned table onto Daggett. The man had gone backward in his chair, and his legs were pinned beneath the table. In a roaring rage, Frío yanked him from beneath it with one arm and hit him across the face with the other, so hard Moore thought it had broken his neck.

He went limp in Frío's grip, and the gross old *bandido* flung him across the room like a sack of grain, to slump, unconscious, against the wall. By this time Ivory had come running from the bedroom in a sleazy wrapper. Her words had been lost in the general sound, but now, as she threw herself down beside Daggett, Moore could hear her again.

"Dad, Dad, what is it, please . . . oh, you've killed him. . . ."

"That *lépero* you call a husband violated my word!" shouted Frío. "The word of Frío Lamar. He and Paint weren't get those cattle from the Skewbar like they claim. It was the Bootjack, and they stop north of the crossing to blot in a Skewbar. *Ruego por mi alma,* that I should get such a *bastardo* for marry my daughter." He turned to Moore, holding out a pleading hand. "You don't think it was me . . . ?"

"All right, all right," said Moore, filled with the bitter, brassy taste of a let-down after that period of intense anger. He took a heavy breath. "Sure, I don't think it was you. I should have known."

"*Bueno. Bueno.*" Frío grinned with that childish shift of

mood. "Let's go in kitchen and get taste of him out of our mouth, hah?"

Paint was standing over against the wall with a sullen look on his face, and Blackeye went about righting the table again, leering at Moore. He said: "You should stay the night, at least. We needed a little salt on the table. Things get too dull out here."

There was a smaller table in the kitchen, and Moore sagged into a chair cut from a great cottonwood stump. With the driving support of all that anger fled from him, the effects of the hard ride were apparent suddenly. He ran a hand through black hair curled tight with sweat, and took the drink of *pulque* Frío offered without comment, gulping it down. He heard Daggett's voice from out there now, weak and irritable, like a whining child. Frío made a toast with his drink, but before he finished it, Ivory came into the kitchen.

"I need some hot water for his head," she told her father, not trying to conceal her anger. "It's all cut up from hitting the wall. Why did you have to do that, Frío?"

His brows shot up. "I tell you. . . ."

"Never mind," she said wearily. "Somebody's coming. We heard a hail from the ridge."

"Probably Sliver with word from Martínez," muttered Frío. "They been locating a new buyer. I be right back, Moore."

VI

Ivory was turned away from Moore, opening a spindle door on her cupboard to pull out a length of cotton and start tearing it in strips. Moore stared at her back, trying to define the vague disturbance in him. There was the poignancy he al-

126

ways felt with sight of her. But something else. The alteration in her. It had been vague, untouchable, the last time he had been here. Now it was more obvious. Her hair was matted and tangled down her back. He had seen her more than once in this wrapper back at her father's house, and could not forget how fully she had filled it. Now, even with it drawn tightly about her, it had a sloppy, slack look. Had she lost that much weight?

"How does it feel to gloat?"

The strained, guttural sound of her voice startled him. "Ivory," he said, helplessly, "don't. . . ."

"Why not?" She wheeled on him, gripping a strip of torn cotton tightly, her eyes blazing. "That's what you came for, isn't it?"

"No. You know what I came for."

"All right. Now you've seen it. Why don't you get out?" For that moment, it had been the old fire in her eyes. But it was dying already, the luster fading until her eyes were as dull, as lifeless, as her hair. He stared at her for a long, tortured space, and then asked in a voice that was barely audible: "Has it been that bad?"

She raised her head again, and her lips parted, as if to speak. For a moment, he saw the tortured look hovering beneath the surface of her eyes. Then she whirled away from him, and he saw her shoulders tremble faintly.

"Get out, Nolan." There was a sob in her voice. "I asked you to get out. . . ."

Before she had finished, the outer door slammed open, and Moore heard the swift shuffle of feet, and then Sliver's voice. "Kynette got Martínez and made him talk. You'd better buy a trunk, Frío. Martínez told him about the island, and Kynette's not far behind me."

Moore felt his whole body grow rigid, and then he had

whirled to jump down the short hallway into the living room, with the sound of Ivory behind him. Sliver stood in the front doorway, wet and dripping from a bad crossing, a wild, frightened look to his scarred face. Daggett was already whirling toward the hall, panic wiping all the swaggering nonchalance from his long face.

"Get some leggings on, Ivory. We're riding. Where'd you put that war bag . . . ?"

"Nobody's riding!" It was Frío's voice, inundating all other sounds. "You're staying here. We're safe as a church. More than three or four horse on that sandbar at a time will crumble it right away. Kynette will put his whole posse on, and the river, she sweep him clear down to Brownsville."

"And we'll be trapped on the island," said Daggett.

"The hell," said Frío. "We can always get off in boats. Maybe the current's so strong nobody else can land here, but all we have to do is push off in a skiff and be carry right down the river to the first spit of mainland."

"You can stay," said Daggett. "Ivory and me are going. I know Kynette. He'll get over here somehow."

"You ain't going take my daughter off, Daggett," said Frío. "If Kynette's that close behind Sliver, you run right into his hands."

"You ain't stopping me," snarled Daggett.

Frío hitched his stag-butted gun around in front of his belly. "Ain't I, Daggett?" he asked.

Moore saw the planes of tension shift across Daggett's back, lifting his weight forward onto his toes. He saw the man's fingers stiffen, and felt his own body gather, thinking Daggett was actually going for it. Then slowly, jerkily, Daggett's weight settled back. His laugh was ragged with its effort.

"Sure, sure, Frío," he said. "I guess I'm just jumpy. Let's

all stay. Safe as a church. That's us."

He tried to swagger to the table, lowering himself into a chair. He poured himself a cup of mescal and tossed it off. Frío stared at him another moment, then turned to put a hand on Blackeye's shoulder.

"You go on out to the shore. If any of the posse get over halfway across the sandbar, haul on that rope we got tied to the dam. When the dam busts, twenty feet of the sandbar will be carry off. They never reach us."

The top of the table blocked off Daggett's hips and legs from Frío, and Moore had started turning toward Ivory, so he only half saw it. A movement of Daggett's hand downward that was so casual it did not catch Moore's full attention. The dull flash of metal in the black shadows cast beneath the table by the lantern above. The roar of a gun. Frío stiffened so spasmodically it looked as if he were trying to jump upward. He swayed, twisting his face farther around to stare in ghastly surprise at Daggett. Another shot crashed, and, from the flame it made beneath the table, Moore realized only now that Daggett had pulled his gun there. Again Frío's body jerked, twisted halfway around, and began to topple.

"Dad!" screamed Ivory.

It jerked Moore from the trance of his surprise with a painful jolt, and he went for his gun. But Paint had been in a position to see what Daggett had done, and his weapon was already out. Instead of whirling toward Moore, he shot the lantern out.

In the sudden darkness, Moore could not shoot for fear of hitting Ivory. He jumped toward Daggett. This time the flame of the gun was the only light, blinding him.

"Daggett," he screamed, "don't be a fool, you'll hit Ivory!"

Again gun sound rocked the room. All the pain in the

world seemed to explode in Moore's elbow. He felt his gun drop from fingers full of numbed agony. The blow of the bullet had enough force to spin him around, and he fell into the wall and slid to the floor in the helpless nausea of the pain, still unable to believe Daggett had done this, with Ivory in the door right behind him.

"Paint?" It was Daggett's voice coming from far off.

"You cross Paint off, Daggett, he's gone to market," said Blackeye, and, before he finished, there was that deafening crash of guns again. Someone screamed in pain. The door swung open violently. Moonlight turned the opening to a saffron rectangle. A body was silhouetted momentarily, plunging out.

Consciousness spinning, Moore pawed desperately around the floor for his gun. He did not know when he became aware of the breathing. At first he thought it was Ivory. Then, with a gradual clearing of his head, he realized it came from in front of him somewhere. There was movement with it, soft, restrained movement. It held a deliberate direction that could not come from a wounded man. It was moving toward Moore. A man with a gun would not have to move. Sliver?

One more chance, Ardiente. Moore could almost hear the man's voice. *I'll give you his whole hide in one strip.* Moore felt tension start its spasmodic twitch through the muscles of his back. Sliver must have heard him go down, screaming at Daggett, placing him from the sound of his voice as he fell. The breathing was nearer now. Sweat began to sting his eyes. Nearer. He tried to hold his own breath. Nearer. . . .

The explosion of movement right in front of him stiffened his whole body. He threw himself aside. He was knocked back against the wall from the hips down by the weight of a body striking him. He heard that Bowie go into adobe with a driving, scraping plunge of steel.

"Damn you!" Sliver's voice escaped him in a gust.

Moore twisted his legs free, kicking viciously at that voice. Sliver howled in pain. Moore kicked again, felt the solid crunch of flesh and bone. He sensed the body rolling violently away from him, and followed its direction across the floor, kicking again and again, until it brought up against the opposite wall. He was close enough to know what he was kicking now, and, as Sliver groaned, making a last, feeble effort to rise, Moore finished it completely, with a vicious, brutal kick in the stomach.

He had to lean against the wall above the limp body, then, panting his words out. "Ivory. Get that light in the kitchen. Shove it in here with your toe."

In a moment, it came, a candle in a tin sconce, scraping over the floor. Its circle of light widened, falling across Blackeye first, sprawled dead across the body of Paint, who had gone to market. Slowly, inexorably, that circle of light rippled over Frío Lamar, where he lay almost at the door. Blood covered his great belly with its black portent, and his eyes did not see the ceiling they stared at.

Her face a pallid mask of utter disbelief, Ivory stumbled across the room to her dead father, dropping to her knees beside him. She crouched there a long time before the tears began to come. They rolled soundlessly down her cheeks from those unblinking eyes. Moore had reached her by then. Somehow, he could not feel the agony of that smashed elbow any more. Somehow, he could only remember that belching, childish, bellowing old scoundrel who had become so close to him in their time together at the Bootjack. It felt as if someone had tied a peal around his guts and pulled it up tight.

Then he found himself staring out the door. He sensed

Ivory's eyes on him, and turned toward her. She must have
read the terrible, growing impulse in him, and he could not
mistake the expression on her face. It was a complete, mu-
tual, tacit understanding.

"He's your husband, Ivory," he said in an empty, hollow
voice.

Her words were as empty, and as terrible. "Not any more,
Nolan."

Hokey Pokey made a great smashing clatter through the
first brush outside the clearing around the house. Each hoof
that hit the ground sent a new jar of pain through that shat-
tered elbow. Moore knew there was only one way out, and did
not bother trailing Daggett, although sign was plain enough
where he had smashed through the thickets, taking short cuts
off the trail through the scattered cattle in the valley and up
onto high ground again. Then he sighted smoke, crossing a
clearing on the downslope ahead. The crash of a shot came.
Moore ducked a post-oak branch, unable to pull his gun and
rein with only one hand.

A *ramadero* of mesquite loomed up ahead with no hole
torn through it. A thinner portion of chaparral was rent fifty
yards to the side, where Daggett had been forced to veer in
order to get through. Moore drove Hokey Pokey straight into
the mesquite Daggett had avoided. With that unerring in-
stinct, the horse pointed toward the most penetrable spot.
There was a great rending crash of brush. Huddled over with
his eyes wide open, Moore had a moment when he thought he
would be torn off. Then they were through.

"Now, who's a brush buster," he found himself snarling.

Daggett had lost precious time avoiding that mesquite and
veering aside to hunt an easier way through, and he was just
disappearing ahead as Moore burst free on this side. Moore

prayed for it to happen just once more, and then lay forward on his horse as Daggett threw one smashing shot at Moore before the brush swallowed him.

Moore followed at a headlong charge, agrito biting like daggers, the honey of huajilla sweeping over him in a heady tide, a post-oak branch barely missing his head. Then, a hundred yards ahead, Moore saw it. Daggett had come up against a *ramadero* of chaparral. There was a torn place in it where he must have tried to plunge through—and failed. For Smoke was reared back on his haunches, chest streaming blood. Daggett heard Moore crashing through mesquite behind, and whirled in the saddle to fire. The gun must have been emptied, for there was no crash of a shot.

Daggett flung the gun from him with a desperate motion, and wheeled Smoke left to run down the line of brush toward a thinner patch. At the same time he switched rein hands so he could pull his other gun, but he reached that thin patch by the time he got the weapon out, and was too busy swerving Smoke into the thicket to make his shot count. It went wild.

Remembering how the land lay here, Moore charged right on into that chaparral Daggett had failed to penetrate. There was a ridge to the left of both men that would force Daggett to veer right back beyond this thicket, until he was crossing the same sector he would have hit if he had come out from this very chaparral.

Again Moore gave Hokey Pokey his head, and the horse changed leads to make a sharp turn right. Moore could not help his fearful gasp. In that last moment, he thought the animal's judgment had finally failed. The chaparral here looked as solid as rock. But with a faith and teamwork born through years of smashing the brush, Moore did not haul up on the reins. He went into it doubled forward, eyes open, waiting to be torn off. But he wasn't. Hokey Pokey's uncanny brush sense had picked a thin patch, and they went through like poking a hole in cheesecloth. There was a blind moment of tearing chaparral and ripping agrito and stabbing Spanish dagger. Then they burst into the open beyond.

Daggett had made it through that other patch fifty yards to the left an instant earlier. But the ridge had forced him back this way, and, as Moore came out of the brush, he almost rode the man down. Daggett reared up in the saddle with surprise, trying to bring his gun up in time. Moore didn't even try for his own weapon. Hokey Pokey's heavy chest went into Smoke's ribs before Daggett's gun was in line, and Moore threw himself bodily over his own horse's head, going into Daggett. The two of them went over with Smoke as it lost balance under Hokey Pokey's charging weight.

Daggett screamed from a pinned leg. Then Smoke had rolled off, and he was trying to scramble erect. Thrown beyond by his jump, Moore rolled to his feet and threw himself back at Daggett. The man still held his gun. Moore caught it by the barrel, twisting it from Daggett's hand. Daggett was rising from his knees, and Moore had that last look at the man's twisted, panicky face, before he struck at it with the butt of the gun.

When he got back to the *jacal,* Moore found that Ivory had packed her father onto the back of a horse. She met him at the door, a dull, apathetic look to her eyes.

"Lee?" she said, in a flat voice.

"I caught him," Moore told her. "Let's forget it now. It was for Frío."

She nodded, face expressionless. Apparently all capacity for emotion had been shocked from her. Moore knew the pain would come later—for both of them.

"I'd like to bury him in the river," she said. "Before Kynette gets here."

He got her a horse and, riding the windblown Hokey Pokey, led the animal carrying Frío's dead body back over the trail, carefully avoiding the spot where he had killed Daggett, until they reached the beach. There was as yet no sign of Kynette. They crossed the shifting sandbar and gained the mainland, turning downriver to the bluffs. Here they weighted Frío's body with rocks and consigned him to the river he had spent his life with. From the bluffs now, they could just make out the first of the posse pushing off into the river. Martínez must have been with them, for they were following the sandbar.

"He's putting too many horses on at once," she said. "He'll never make it."

"He'll find some way," Moore told her. "I know Kynette. But it won't do him any good now."

"Nolan . . ." she said, staring up at him, "I was wrong about so many things."

"There's no need to talk about them," he said. "Except the way I felt tonight. You *were* wrong about that. I wasn't gloating. I'll never do that. Or say I told you so. Frío was right. We've got to learn ourselves. If you've learned, that's enough."

"You held me in your arms once, Nolan," she told him. "I need that very much now. Will you do it again?"

Valley of Secret Guns

This short novel was completed by Les Savage, Jr., in February, 1945. It was sold to Fiction House that same month. The author was paid $380.00 at 2¢ a word. It appeared as "Valley of Secret Guns" in *Lariat Story Magazine* (9/45). This is its first publication in book form.

I

They were watching him now. Well, hadn't he expected that? Wasn't it always that way at first? Yet, moving toward them, he felt it was different than before, somehow. Nothing tangible, nothing in their faces, or their movements. Yet different. It gave him a small, growing apprehension, but it gave him a certain satisfaction. The Double Shank should be different. Hadn't all the other spreads been the same, for so long? Hadn't he hunted long enough? It was about time he found it, this way.

"Boys, I want you to meet Bob Tulare. He's our new buster while Eddie's laid up." It was Albert Pierce introducing him, owner of the Double Shank, big and heavy and thick-fleshed around the jowls with good living. "Tulare, this is Danny Lonoke, our ramrod."

Danny Lonoke? Six feet tall maybe, with a set of gut hooks on his spike-heeled boots that looked fit to rip the tripe right out of a horse with one rake. He must have just been working the horses because his gun wasn't around his lean belly, and Tulare didn't see how the man's Levi's stayed up around his negligible hips without a belt. He was looking at Tulare out of dark eyes that held no expression, and his thin lips barely moved when he spoke.

"Glad to know you, Tulare."

"Likewise," said Tulare, and felt their eyes on him like a physical weight. It shouldn't have made him feel that way. Hadn't he contract-busted enough bronchos before? Hadn't he hit almost every spread in this section of New Mexico? He should be used to meeting new crews this way by now. He was lean and young, Tulare, in old blue jeans that might have stood alone when he took them off at night, his thick red hair hanging long down his neck from beneath a battered, flat-topped hat, his face pink with the perpetual sunburn of the light-complexioned man who would never tan, a faint spray of freckles on his snub nose.

"This is Henry Desha, best all-'round roper you'll find anywhere," Pierce was going on, "and Honest John. . . ."

"Right pleased to shake hands with you, boy," said Honest John, and held out his left hand, and Tulare felt a smile broaden his mouth, because Honest John was the first one to do that.

He was a little weazened ranny, Honest John, but the grip of his gnarled hand bore a surprising strength, and a warmth, and he was smiling, too, revealing how few tobacco-stained teeth he had left in his gums. When he had finished shaking hands, Honest John shoved his old black hat back on a pate as bald as a slick horn and squinted one of his faded blue eyes at Tulare's spurless boots.

"If you're going to top the bronc's we've got here, you'll need a pair of gut hooks for them Hyers of yours. There's some hanging on the fence here, I reckon."

"I'll leave you with the boys," Albert Pierce told Tulare. "Maybe come down later in the day and see how you work."

Pierce tried to hide his glance at Tulare's armless right shoulder, and couldn't, and then turned uncomfortably back toward the sprawling adobe house in front of a meadow of stirrup-high blue root that rose into a low roll of piñon-studded hills. The crew began to shift with that same discomfort. Tulare stood there a moment longer, facing their stiff gazes, then moved toward the fence. There was some gear slung on the opera seat, a pair of bat-wings and several coils of hemp and two or three sets of spurs. He chose a pair of Texas rowels and squatted down to strap them on his boots.

He sensed the movement of Lonoke toward him, and spoke without looking up. "Pulled one of my gut hooks apart on a roan's cinch over Carlsbad way last week. Been meaning to pick me up a new pair."

"We don't mind the spurs," said Lonoke. "You use them as long as you're here if you want," and he was studying Tulare from those enigmatic eyes. "Just what are you here for, Tulare?"

Tulare raised his head, and his sun-bleached eyebrows rose. "I'm a contract buster. I thought your *caporal* made it clear. You need a bunch of new bronc's busted to fill out your strings for spring roundup? I'm here to do it."

"I mean what else?"

Tulare had his spurs strapped on, and he stood up, not quite as tall as Lonoke, or as broad through the shoulders. "Nothing else, Lonoke. Why?"

"The name seems familiar."

"I've been working Eddy County a couple of years."

"Something else." Lonoke shook his head, then dismissed it with a shrug. He let his dark eyes fall on Tulare's left shoulder. "I guess I might as well speak what's in all our minds. How do you peel a bronc'?"

Tulare felt a relief that it was out, finally. "I never did use my arms to ride a horse."

Perhaps Lonoke took that personally, for the first flush crept into his face. "I never saw a one-armed flash-rider before."

"You're seeing one now," said Tulare, and grinned, because this was not different now, this was what he had become used to.

Lonoke spread his feet suddenly, and hunched his broad shoulders forward a little, as if to meet something, and his lips hardly moved over his words. "I don't want any trouble, Tulare. If you're here to break our rough string, all right. But if you're here for something else, you'd better not stay."

This was part of it, then? Tulare felt a strange, tingling sensation begin down inside of him, and he tried to read what lay behind the enigma of Lonoke's eyes, and couldn't. It *was* different, then, the Double Shank, it was different from all the other spreads he had seen, and was this part of it, Lonoke's warning?

"Don't threaten me, Lonoke," he said. "Whatever I'm here for, don't threaten me."

Lonoke reached out and grabbed his shirt front, jerking Tulare forward and off balance. "I'm not threatening you, Tulare, I'm telling you. I'm ramrod here, and I don't want any trouble. If you don't understand that. . . ."

Lonoke's sharp cry cut his own voice off, and his jump backward was a spasmodic reaction to the pain of Tulare's spur biting into his shin. Tulare had hooked the man like he would a broncho, and he put his foot back down carefully, looking at the rip in the leg of Lonoke's Levi's, just above his boot top, blood already beginning to redden the torn edges of the denim. Lonoke stood with his hand still held out in the position it had been to grip Tulare's shirt. He dropped it suddenly, and Tulare saw his intent plain in his black eyes.

"Lonoke!" Tulare's voice was a whip, and it stopped Lonoke there, bent forward slightly. "I told you not to threaten me. You may rod this crew, but I didn't sign on with them. I contracted to bust your *caporal*'s horses at five bucks a bust, and Pierce is the only man I answer to for that. I'll answer you, but it won't be the same. If you think having lost a wing makes me any different than other men, come ahead. You won't get that spur up your leg the second time. You'll get it in your teeth!"

They had thrown a pied broncho and blinded it with a bandanna and were cinching a slick-fork Cheyenne on its back. Tulare bent through the bars and moved toward them stiffly, feeling Lonoke's eyes on him all the way. Honest John finished tightening the latigo and stepped back as they let the blinded broncho up, quivering and snorting.

Honest John turned to grin at Tulare. "You're the first man I ever saw face down Danny Lonoke that way, boy. What you got?"

"Maybe he didn't like the idea of chewing on Texas rowels," said Tulare.

The old man's grin faded. "You shouldn't have done it, really, boy. Lonoke isn't a nice man to cross. I don't think he's afraid of you. You might have backed him down there, but I don't think he's afraid of you. I don't think he's afraid of anything."

"He seemed to think I was here for something else besides bronc' snapping."

"Ain't you?"

Tulare felt the small, tingling sensation down in his loins again, and he studied Honest John. They knew? He turned toward the horse suddenly, angered at his own apprehension. What if they did? He wanted them to know. Suddenly he felt a savage desire that they should know. If this was it, he wanted them all to know why. He jerked on the cinch viciously, found it solid, then whirled back to Honest John.

"I guess you're right."

Honest John held up his hand, grinning sheepishly. "Never mind, boy. I think we're all a little touchy today, that's all. Lonoke and me and everybody. He just don't trust any new hand since that cattle business started last month."

"Oh." Tulare suddenly realized how close he had come to slipping, and the grip he held on himself now was almost physical pain. "Cattle business?"

"Yeah. If you been working this section, you know. The same way it happened to Edward Alden's Flying W last year, and the Box H before that. Ordinary rustling on the surface. But nobody can do anything about it. County lawmen, state badges, even government marshals."

Tulare turned to tug at the latigo on the pied horse's rig so Honest John couldn't see his face. He'd thrown his tree on the right cayuse then. The Double Shank. Started already.

"Never heard of rustlers that slick," he said. "Sooner or later they leave some sign."

"Oh, these rannies leave plenty of sign," chuckled Honest John. "They don't sprout wings and fly the cattle away. But whenever the lawmen hook onto the trail, it's so old they can't foller it for beans, and it don't lead them no place anyhow. All the time those rustlers been operating here, nobody's ever found one hot trail on them."

"I always figured, if you can't sit one end of the kak, you should try the other," said Tulare. "How about the brand inspectors? Just as many bad-hats have been caught when an inspector traced a decorated brand back to them as have been snagged by a posse trailing them. If these rustlers have been working as long as you say, they must have passed a lot of cattle through the chutes. Inspector's bound to spot a changed brand sooner or later."

"I'll agree twice as many rustlers have been nabbed since they put in brand inspectors as before," said Honest John, "but that dally don't hog-tie this cow. Not one blotted brand has been reported on the outfits these boys have taken cattle off of."

"The border?"

"You think that many cattle could be sold on the wet market below the border without some word of it leaking back here? You know they couldn't. Years it's been going on, and, so far, nobody knows where they go with the cattle or what they do with them when they get there."

"You afraid of that horse?"

At first Tulare thought Honest John had said it. Then he turned to see Henry Desha, standing there. Desha had moved around from the other side of the broncho's head, still holding the blind on with one hand, his other hand gripping the cheek-piece. He was a stubby little man with leather leggings Mexicans called *chivarras* on his horse-collar legs, and a short spade beard that didn't quite manage to hide the ugliness of his thick-lipped, rather sensuous mouth. Best all-'round roper you'll find anywhere, Pierce had remarked about him.

"You must be hard up for kaks," said Tulare, looking at the slick fork. "Or did Lonoke suggest you hang this one on?"

"Don't you like it?" Desha's grin wasn't nice.

"Go on," Honest John poked Tulare in the ribs, chuckling. "You know Lonoke put them up to cinching this slick fork saddle on the bronc'. He's out to make it as hard as he can for you after what you did. But you can top this bronc', slick fork or anything. Just climb in that kak and bite his kidneys with your can openers and you're off. Why I never used a bronc' saddle in my life. That crazy high fork was always knocking me in the chin. Fact is, I never really liked to scissor a horse with a hull at all. I did most of my breaking naked. Just tie a rope on its nose and let me climb on top and there isn't any bronc' from here to the Mizzou I can't peel. I busted over a hundred in one day, all bareback. They had 'em all lined up outside the corral, shooting them in one side all wild and savage and snorting, and dragging them out the other as gentle as newborn dogies. I broke them so fast they didn't even have to close the gates. I'd stand up on the opera seat at one side of the corral, and they'd bulge a bronc' in and I'd jump onto his back and break him so quick he didn't know which end his tail was hooked on, and then I'd jump up on the top rail of the other side and be ready for the next bronc'."

"Oh, shut up," said Desha. "You never broke a horse in your life."

Honest John turned to him, a hurt look deepening the wind wrinkles around his pale eyes. "Are you implying, Henry, that I wasn't telling the truth?"

Desha threw back his ugly, scarred head and let out a raucous laugh, and then that was cut off abruptly, and he looked at Tulare, and his face was dark. "Get in that tree or I'm going to let the critter go right now."

Tulare reached up and twisted the stirrup around, facing toward the horse's rump. He felt Desha's eyes on him from behind, and the sense of something began growing inside him. Then he saw how Honest John was backing away, an odd, new expression crossing his wrinkled face. One-armed that way, Tulare had to hold the stirrup till his foot was in it and then grab the saddle and pull himself up. He understood what it was now, and guessed it would come when he let go the stirrup and reached for the kak. He was still grasping the stirrup, with his foot in it, and he set himself. Then, with a violent grunt, his hand left the oxbow and darted for the saddle, and he was jumping upward. Even as he swung, he heard Desha shout, and half saw the man's leap backward, the blind coming off in his hand. If he hadn't been expecting it, Tulare would have been thrown backward by the horse's first plunging leap even before he had gotten into the saddle. But his violent swing had cast his leg over the saddle before the horse went forward, and he found the other stirrup with his free foot, grabbing for the reins.

"It tore loose!" shouted Desha, jumping backward. "The hoss tore loose!"

Tulare knew it hadn't. But he was in the leather now, and it boiled over, and with the first buck he knew what kind of a beast they had put him on. There was something vicious about the way it bogged its head, even before it hit the top. Tulare yanked the reins high to pull its head back up, and it struck with all four legs stiff as pokers, and his own legs shuddered beneath him with the jar.

When the piebald broncho realized Tulare was still on, it gave a crazed squeal and started to weave. Tulare had ridden pioneer buckers before, but never one that took off with such a virulent malignance in its every jarring plunge. The pied animal's hoofs never struck the ground in a straight line, and its turbulent, weaving motion was calculated to unbalance Tulare with every jump. He had to keep jerking his body back and forth, side to side, striving to follow the horse's motion with the center of his own balance. His insides were juggled till they felt like jelly and his head was roaring and the corral spun before his eyes.

"Put on your grappling irons!" shouted Honest John from where he had taken a seat on the top rail. "That pied devil's a killer, boy. He's a cinch-binder. If you don't rake him out of that weaving, he'll fall back on you. Dig him!"

The pied broncho had already begun to rear up, but Tulare knocked him back down with his fist, raking him at the same time. Unable to pull a fall-back, the horse began to spin. Almost blind now with the jarring, Tulare was trying to feel it more than see, because he sensed what would follow the spin. Suddenly the horse went up forward, and Tulare was already kicking free. He struck the ground on both feet, and then hit on the soft part of his buttocks, rolling off on a shoulder, and, even as he struck, the horse had turned over in mid-air and come down with its legs up and its saddle on the bottom. A man sticking to the leather would have been crushed beneath it.

Tulare rolled away from the animal as it scrambled to its feet, dazed by its own fall. With another frenzied whinny, it lowered its head, spinning around crazily to smash up against the corral fence. The jar knocked Honest John off, and he fell on over the plunging horse to the ground. Yet he got to his feet quickly, yelling at Desha.

"Get your clothesline out! This killer's so lathered he's liable to do anything!"

Desha already had his rope going, and he slung it in a hooley-ann past Honest John. But the cunning pied broncho jerked aside from the small loop. It smashed again into the fence, and then Honest John's running figure caught its eye, and it wheeled and charged him. Desha had snaked his rope back again, and he tried to forefoot the animal, but the piebald danced out of the loop.

"Snag him!" shouted Honest John hoarsely, stumbling on across the corral. "I thought you was a roper. Get him on this next throw, damn you, or my name's Dead John!"

The maddened animal had quartered John to cut him off before he reached the fence. Desha was desperately trying to snake in his rope for that last try, but Tulare was already running toward him.

"Get out of the way, you damned, one-armed . . . !"

That was all Desha got out before Tulare grabbed the rope from his hands and shouldered him aside so hard he stumbled backward and fell. The broncho was almost on John, thirty feet across the corral, its crazed screams drowning out John's shouts. Then Tulare had his rope snaked in, and he made the toss. It wasn't up in the air, the way Desha had been throwing. It was what the Mexicans called a *mangana de pie*, shooting up from below so the animal wouldn't spot the rope spinning in the air, the loop forming a figure eight, the upper half snaking over the horse's neck, the lower part snagging the churning forefeet. Tulare had his end snubbed around his own waist, and he was yanked forward violently as the horse went down, the ground shaking beneath his hoofs. When the dust had settled enough to see the horse's kicking hoofs, Tulare let the rope slack, and sent a roll down its length that snagged another hitch around its hind legs. By that time, the hand named Kensington and several others had reached the animal with peals. The horse had fallen within three feet of Honest John, and the old man stood there a long time, watching Kensington hobble and blind the piebald. Finally John shook his head dazedly, and walked around the animal and came toward Tulare.

"I guess I owe you some sort of thanks," he said shakily. "I ain't been so near to riding my last horse since Wild Bill

Hickok's gun misfired with its business end against my head."

"Next time you want me to top a crazy killer," said Tulare, "tell me beforehand, and we won't have to knock him down with a rope."

They had taken the snorting, quivering animal back to the chute, and Kensington came across the corral, a tall, bow-legged youth with an easy smile on his dark face, hands tucked into the waistband of beltless jeans. He was looking past Tulare, and Tulare glanced that way. Desha was standing by the fence, sullenly brushing dirt off the seat of his pants.

"You got a perfect score so far," said Kensington in a soft, amused voice. "Only been on the Double Shank an hour, and already the ramrod and the top roper are willing to cut out your guts with their Barlow knives the first chance they get."

The pied broncho had dazed itself with its own frenzy, crashing up against the fence and falling on its back that way, and there would be no telling whether it was actually broken for several days.

No matter how consummate a man was busting the rough ones, he still felt beaten and stiff at the end of a day like this, and, when they called it off at dusk, with seven busted bronchos in the corral, Tulare was willing enough. The cook shack was apart from the bunkhouse, a long frame building that had been put up later than the adobe structures, its single table consisting of two planks set on a pair of tall sawbucks.

"The cook's out on a drunk again," Honest John told Tulare. "Every Monday after payday we have to dish up our own beans cold. You'll find a tin plate over by the stove."

The old man was the only one who spoke to Tulare. Lonoke sat at the end of the table, beans untouched, watching Tulare with a tight-lipped intensity. Tulare finished his beans and cold coffee, and leaned back.

"I'm turning in early. Got a free bunk?"

"One at the end of the shack," said Honest John. "There's a lantern hanging by the door. First hand in usually lights it."

Tulare had dumped his sougan up by the main house, and he had to go up there before going to the bunkhouse. He came back with a tarp under his arm and shoved back the door of the bunkhouse, fumbling around in the darkness for the lantern. From the cook shack farther on came the muffled sound of someone talking, and then a short laugh. It must have been the lantern that made the metallic sound when his hand struck it; he didn't have time to find out. There was another sound, a shuffling, rasping sound. Tulare was turning toward it when he sensed the violent movement from somewhere behind him, and he threw himself to one side. The blow struck his shoulder with a stunning force, and he cried out with the pain.

His body, falling into the wall, shook the whole building, and dislodged a shower of the dried, flaky *yeso* they white-washed their adobe interiors with. Choking on the flakes and dust of the *yeso,* he thrust himself away from the wall in time to meet the other man's next rush. Tulare sensed the blow more than saw it, and ducked in under with his good arm. The man grunted with having missed Tulare, and then his heavy body crashed into the fist Tulare had thrown out there, and his grunt turned to a gasp of pain. Tulare threw himself on in, grappling the man with his arm. He slashed back and forth with his feet in a sideways kick. The other man shouted something as those spurs caught him, and tried to jump away, but Tulare held him in with his arm about his sweating torso and shifted his weight to kick deeper with his other foot.

That one knocked the man's feet from under him, and he

149

fell away from Tulare. Tulare tried to jump him in the dark, but the man rolled toward the door and scrambled to his feet, his body a dim blot in the open portal, going out. Tulare stumbled over the lantern he had knocked off its peg, trying to follow the man, and went to his knees with a bitter curse. By the time he had risen and run outside, there was no one in sight. Tulare's voice was hardly audible in the night, as he stood there, breathing heavily.

"Lonoke?"

II

Forty-Rod Farnum sat with his back against a big red rock, a great, gross man with a belly that lowered in folds between enormous thighs that had long ago split out the seams of his ancient blue jeans. He was hatless, and perfectly bald, and his jowls bulged red and veined on either side of a bulbous nose that shone like a bull's-eye lantern, and his bloodshot eyes were almost hidden by the rolls of fat forming his cheeks. He was holding a big jug up in one hand and talking to the enormous mare that stood cropping at some bunchgrass in front of him.

"You execrable equine," he said, "you boorish bidet. I have fed you on the fat of the land and housed you in a manner befitting an emperor's charger. I have hung on you trappings a queen herself would envy. I have stayed awake ten nights in a row nursing your encephalomyelitis. I have worried myself into hysterics over your pododermatitis. I have treated you more tenderly than a mother would treat her child. And now you perpetrate this facinorous peccability." Forty-Rod hiccoughed, stopped to take a swig from the jug, then turned back to the horse. "Come here, you

Mephistophelean miscreant. I would get back on."

The man must have been sitting the saddle there a long time, near the horse-maimer cactus, chuckling to himself, but Forty-Rod only now became aware of him. He lowered the jug, trying to focus his bloodshot eyes. "Ah," he said finally, "Veracious John. How fortunate you should pass this way. By some iniquitous mischance I have lost contact with yonder bucolic quadruped, and, if you could be persuaded to help me mount again, I might give you a taste of the untrammeled joy this jug contains."

"You mean you're so drunk you fell out of the tree and can't climb on again," said Honest John, gigging his whey-bellied *chopo* horse toward Forty-Rod. "You know I never could lift you back in your kak again. I'll just get down and rest my hocks a while to make it even." He swung stiffly to the ground and lowered himself to his hunkers, contemplating the jug. "That new bronc'-scratcher came in yesterday. Bob Tulare. I never saw such a ranny. He blew one of his wings somewhere, but he peels those wild ones better than any man with two arms I ever saw. He rode that pied killer into the ground before it threw him. Had to spin to do it. And rope? You ought to see Tulare sling that cat-gut. Henry Desha can't touch him. Tulare saved my life with it. You know how that piebald gits wild and tries to kill everything in sight. After it tossed Tulare, it got after me. Desha had two tries at it and got hornswoggled every one. Then Tulare grabbed Desha's clothesline and threw the neatest *mangana* you ever want to see. Forefooted the piebald just before he caught me up against a fence. I wouldn't be hunkered here now if it wasn't for that one-armed boy."

"Oh, now contain your propensities, my prevaricating companion," said Forty-Rod. "We aren't going to have that difficulty again."

"I sorter liked the boy."

Forty-Rod burped disgustedly. "I might have known it. I remember the last time you took a liking to a man. It cost us no end of trouble. I won't have it, John. If you must have an outlet for your sentimentality, confine it to Sometime or myself. Haven't we afforded you an ample amount of bosom companionship? Haven't we caroused our misguided lives away by your side? Haven't we sympathized with your infamous predilection for prevarication? Who else would give you such friendship?"

"Tulare had a fight with Lonoke," said Honest John, looking up at the sky. "Faced Lonoke down, too. Don't that put him on our side?"

Forty-Rod took another swig, grimaced. "I can't see anyone facing Lonoke down. He just let his intelligence control his natural instincts. How would it look to the crew for a ramrod with all his members to engage in fisticuffs with a one-armed man?"

"I thought of that," said Honest John. "But I think Lonoke would have held off, one arm or two. You didn't see that red-headed bronc'-scratcher, Forty-Rod. When he gets going, you forget he only packs one wing. At first I thought Lonoke crossed Tulare through being so touchy about this cattle business. Lonoke's had fights with more than one of us these last months. He was all lathered up about you not getting back in time to cook Monday hash, too. Then Desha put a bug in my ear. He claims Lonoke figured Tulare was something more than just a bronc'-peeler."

Forty-Rod rolled a bloodshot eye toward John. "What do you figure?"

Honest John rubbed his leg. "I don't know. Tulare's hard to make out. Some things fit. Others don't. Somebody jumped him in the bunk shack last night when the rest of us was at the cook shack. He put his grappling irons into them the same way he did Lonoke. You ever fought a man that uses his spurs that way?"

"No," said Forty-Rod. "Have you?"

"Right effective," said Honest John. "Tulare don't fool around. He lets a man know right off. I guess Lonoke knows it."

"Tulare . . . Tulare. . . ." Forty-Rod seemed to be contemplating. "Wasn't there a Tulare who owned the Single Bar about ten, twelve years back?"

"Terwilliger," said Honest John. "That forty-rod is affecting your memory."

Forty-Rod shook his head. "Tulare. I'm sure of it. He could have had a son."

"We'd remember a one-armed boy. You're putting your latigo through the wrong catch ring. You better finish that jug off now. Lonoke and Kensington aren't far behind me. We came out to try and cut some rustler sign. Another bunch of steers was cut out of the north herd over Saturday. Desha just came in this morning with the news. The rest of the hands are as jumpy as spooked fillies. Lonoke is buggy as a cow with bots."

"Here is our ubiquitous ramrod now," said the fat man, nodding toward the two horsebackers who had just rounded the turn in the trail.

Danny Lonoke's face was flushed angrily as he swung off his big chestnut. "I thought I told you to ride that ridge north," he told Honest John. "I'm getting fed up with you Flying W 'pokes. Been here a month and think you own the whole pasture."

Honest John stood up slowly. "We ain't the only hands came to you when the Flying W folded, Lonoke."

"Get back on that whey-bellied plug of yours and see if

you can't cut some sign along the ridge top like I told you," said Desha.

"That ain't no plug," said Honest John. "It's an honest to goodness *chopo* horse. I got him in Carlsbad last year. I paid nine hundred and fifty iron men for him, and that was cheap."

"Nine hundred and fifty bucks?" The black-haired foreman was holding his natural ebullience in with some effort now, face dark, lips working across his teeth. "You never had one buck all together in your life."

"One buck!" Honest John's weazened face took on a hurt expression. "Now, Lonoke, you know that's not true. Why, in the old days, I was the richest rancher in this section. I had a mansion up by Lincoln County. A hundred rooms in it. Two hundred Navajo servants to do just what I wanted. So many cattle I couldn't count them. I used to keep ten thousand dollars in gold in the bottom of my dresser just for pocket money. I wore gold spurs and rode a gold-plated Porter saddle and the *chopo* horse I had then cost me five thousand dollars even. . . ."

"All right, all right," said Lonoke. "I've heard your windies before."

"Why, Lonoke," said Forty-Rod, "do you mean to insinuate that Honest John is undeserving of his sobriquet?"

"Keep out of this, fat man," said Lonoke. "If I don't see you back at that cook shack tonight, you might as well take your frying pan to another spread."

"Fat man!" Forty-Rod tried to get up but couldn't quite make it, and sank back, hiccoughing. "I will admit I am slightly oleaginous. But fat! You have insulted us both now, Lonoke. You have intimated that Honest John is not the height of unperjured rectitude, and you have badly declared that I carry more avoirdupois than is actually necessary. . . ."

"That's all." Lonoke had moved up to Honest John, and his lips barely moved across his words. "I'm asking you once more, are you going to get on that boneyard of yours?"

"No," said Honest John. "Not till you apologize. Nobody ever doubted my word before, and it hurts me. I. . . ."

"Damn you!" Shouting it, Lonoke caught the old man by his collar and spun him around toward the horse. Stumbling to keep from falling, Honest John twisted around and caught Lonoke's hand. The strength of his grip must have surprised Lonoke, because his mouth opened suddenly, and he let go of the old man's collar. Then he swung around the other way with his free left arm, catching Honest John on the side of the head. It knocked John back against his horse, and Lonoke jumped after him. Forty-Rod saw Honest John go for his gun. He had it halfway out when Lonoke reached him. The foreman caught his gun arm in one hand, bellying up against Honest John. Holding the man's gun in its holster that way, Lonoke drew back his free fist for the blow, and Forty-Rod saw what it would do.

"Keep your hand right there," said Forty-Rod.

Lonoke stiffened, his fist growing white at the knuckles, still held in mid-air. Then, holding Honest John that way, he twisted his head around to look at Forty-Rod. The fat man sat where he had been, and in one hand he still held the whisky jug, but in the other he had an ugly little stingy gun. "That's right," he told Lonoke, "and now I think you'd better let go of my old friend, unless you want me to be the cause of an aperture in your head that wouldn't match your ears."

Eddy County west of the Pecos was up to its stirrup leathers in spring grass, and the porcupine cactus was blooming yellow along the bare ridges. The bright-crested *paisanos* kept flashing out of the skunk-brush. Getting Forty-

Rod Farnum onto his mare had been a task as monumental as the man himself, but now he sat comfortably ensconced in the custom-built saddle from the Porter shop in Texas, girths creaking peevishly with each shift of his ponderous weight, the mare plodding stolidly along through the acrid dust. Honest John rode by his side, Lonoke and Kensington trotting ahead. Honest John was chuckling and scratching his gray stubble.

"That's the second time in as many days Lonoke's been hornswoggled," he said. "If the end of that stingy gun you pack didn't look so big, I think he would have jumped you and stuffed it down your throat, chunk of lead and all."

"What does our volatile ramrod think he will find out here?" said Forty-Rod Farnum, tilting the jug up to his lips.

"Cattle sign," said Honest John. "He found where the bunch had been cut from the north herd, and we're follering the tracks now."

Forty-Rod took the jug down, frowning at it. "How interesting. Does he think he'll find anything different than the last time?"

Honest John rubbed his back, squinting at the sky. "My sciatica hurts. That means rain or trouble. I hope it's rain."

Forty-Rod shook the jug, cocking his head to ascertain what he was afraid had happened. "And where were you when all this bovine appropriation was going on?"

"Me?" said John. "Why, I was busting the bronc's up at the house when this bunch of steers was cut out. Where were you?"

"Saturday night? Now what a foolish interrogation. You know where I am every Saturday night in the year. A hundred men at the Carlsbad Saloon must have seen me partaking." Forty-Rod shook his head mournfully, dropping the jug reluctantly. "These containers don't hold the same gallon they used to."

Up ahead, Lonoke stopped his big dun abruptly and swung down, hunkering over something in the scattered drop-seed. "This is it," he said finally, and jerked his head toward the ridge of their flank. "Took them down that talus till they wanted to turn west. Looks like they're heading toward the river."

He cast a sullen look toward Honest John, then mounted his horse. They rode on, Lonoke bent out of his saddle to see the marks of the driven cattle in the soft ground, and Honest John hunched over on his whey-bellied nag.

"See what you've done now, Forty-Rod. I'd rather put my hand on a sidewinder than have Lonoke look at me that way. Next time he won't give you a chance to get that stingy gun out. He'll just open up and send us all to hell on a shutter. I know him."

"My veracious friend," said Forty-Rod, "you don't mean to tell me you are afraid of Danny Lonoke?"

"Afraid?" Honest John bridled. "I ain't afraid of any man. I could still whip Lonoke, old as I am. Why, when me and Davy Crockett was fighting in the Alamo . . ."—the shot cut him off, and he stiffened in the saddle, his voice hoarse and cracked when it could be heard again—"trouble. I knew it. My sciatica hurt. I knew it."

The horses were whinnying and rearing, and Forty-Rod Farnum knew he couldn't maintain his precarious seat on the spooked mare much longer, so he picked a soft spot as he hit, and then rolled into some buckthorn.

He had enough padding to provide for an exigency like this, and, when he sat up, it wasn't his bony structure in which he felt what pain he had. The buckthorn had scratched his bald pate, and he sat there, dabbing vaguely at the blood which persistently trickled into one eye, watching the other men out of the other eye. Lonoke and Kensington had left their horses, one way or the other, and were sprawled out behind the rocks farther down the gully. Lonoke had a Winchester he'd snatched from its scabbard under his stirrup leather, and he kept moving his head around tentatively, trying to see who was potting at them from above. Honest John crawled up to where Forty-Rod sat like a bleary-eyed Buddha behind the buckthorn.

"That iniquitous ingrate," Forty-Rod told him, "that maleficent marplot. This is the second time I've lost my saddle today. I'm going up there and put my stingy gun between his teeth and shoot his bicuspids out the nether extremity of his duodenum."

He got his .50 caliber Krider Derringer out from beneath his dirty red vest and stared crawling out from behind the buckthorn.

"Don't be a fool!" shouted Lonoke. "You'll get punched so full of holes you won't hold hay. John, stop that fat fool!"

"Ain't no use," Forty-Rod heard John say. "Farnum's mad now. He's drunk and he's mad, and you couldn't hold him back with a twenty-mule team, Lonoke. I just wouldn't want to be on the other end of his stingy gun now, that's all."

Well, maybe he was mad. Forty-Rod ducked placidly behind a small rock and let one of the high-caliber bullets whine over him, and then began crawling up the slope again. Maybe he was mad. He was drunk. He knew that. And nobody was going to unhorse him like that with impunity. Billingsgate barbarians.

He ducked again as the lead whined at him. He had a surprising faculty of making the scant cover suffice for his ponderous bulk, rarely showing himself to whoever was above as he moved inexorably upward. He was sweating profusely now, and that trickle of blood from his ripped pate kept stinging his eye, only adding to his irritation. But he didn't know what real anger was till he reached the ridge and found no one there. He sat down by a rock and began to swear.

Pretty soon the others trailed up, and Honest John hunkered down beside Forty-Rod, chuckling. "I guess they saw you coming and thought it was an army. Did you see who it was?"

"No." Forty-Rod dabbed at his perspiring jowls, and he was looking at the marks across the ridge. "But there are remains."

"So it is, so it is," said Honest John, and moved to squat over some tracks. "Look at that print. I never saw a man in such small boots. It must have been made by a kid."

"A kid," said Forty-Rod Farnum, "or a girl."

III

The cottonwoods sighed mournfully in the breeze, and the tree toads added their ceaseless chirping to the other night sounds. The yellow moon sifted through the foliage and cast dappled shadows across the hairy black cow pony standing there. It was a snuffy little stud, and it kept shifting nervously and pawing at the loose ground. Tulare himself felt nervous. He had wanted a dozen times to light a cigarette. He ran his hand soothingly across the rough coat of the pony, then hitched restlessly at his iron-handled Remington. Suddenly the animal lifted its head, ears stiffening. Tulare felt its neck swell, and he caught the noseband quickly, twisting his hand beneath it to shut the horse's mouth over the whinny.

He couldn't hear it at first. The trees made a black pattern in front of him, and beyond that was Jacarilla Ridge where

Honest John and the others had been shot at the day before. The black pony tried to pull away from Tulare, and he gave a sharp tug on the noseband, forcing its head down. Then he caught the movement out there, dim at first, unreal. He licked his lips, feeling his breath come faster. The shadowy figure became visible, someone leading a horse, stopping every now and then to scan the ground. Tulare had been expecting it and wasn't surprised when that other horse raised its head abruptly and turned toward him, letting out a whinny. Whoever it was stood up, too, pulling at the animal, then stopped to peer toward the trees.

The horse quit jumping around, but the person continued staring at the trees. Then, with a jerk, the figure whirled and mounted. Tulare let go of his pony's noseband and jumped out of the trees, hauling his animal after him.

"Hold it," he shouted, "hold it." Then he saw that would do no good, and turned around and jumped on his own mount. The horse ahead had already been wheeled and was racking off toward the ridge. Tulare dug in his gut hooks, and the black pony shot ahead, the dull drum of its hoofs turning to a staccato beat as they left soft ground and crossed some rock. The mount ahead must have been five-gaited, and its rack was no match for the cow pony's dead run, and Tulare had halved the distance between them by the time they reached rising ground. The other rider cut parallel to the ridge and turned in the saddle, shouting at Tulare.

"Don't come any closer. I've got a gun. Don't be a fool."

The voice sounded shrill and strained. Center-fire rig popping and snapping beneath him, Tulare unhitched his dally. The moonlight gave him a good target, and he didn't have to get too close with forty-five feet of maguey in his hand.

"Haul up," he yelled, "or I'll dab this on you!"

The shot was his answer. He ducked instinctively with the

whine of lead over his head, and then gave his pony a last dig with his Texas rowels and shook out his loop. He never whirled his rope, and his toss was neat and skillful, the loop spreading out behind him and to one side to open just before the throw. He saw the rider ahead try to avoid it, but he had seen cows do that, too, and, when he felt the tug on his maguey, dallied it on his horn. The horse squatted like a jack rabbit, and Tulare was off before it had quit sliding. Trained for cow work, it reared back and stood, stiff-legged, to hold the rope taut from where it was snubbed on the saddle horn to the writhing figure ahead on the ground. The rider had been pulled off the back of that other horse, and the animal had continued running. The rider was rolling around on the ground, trying to tear free of the noose, but the skillful cow pony countered every movement, keeping the rope taut. When he had reached the writhing, belly-down figure, Tulare gave a tug on the rope, and the pony stepped forward to slacken up.

Without trying to get free of the loop, the one on the ground rolled over and jumped erect. Tulare tried to yank more slack and snag the scissoring feet with a roll, but he was knocked backwards by the person's body. In that moment, before he struck the ground, he caught a glimpse of the pale, twisted face above him, and his own shout was hoarse in his ears.

"My God," he said, "you're a girl!"

She had one of her arms free when they hit, clawing at his face. He caught her sinewy little hand and brought one leg up in the air beside her, kicking across her body to roll her over. There was something feral in her scream as she tried to rise above him. Then the weight of his leg took her off balance and threw her over, and he was straddling her. He caught at the rope and pulled it tight and jumped up and back from her,

161

snapping her legs with a loop he rolled out of the slack. With one arm left free, she tried to catch the rope and pull it off her, but he rolled another loop out of slack and caught the free arm. Then he slipped it under one of her wrists held tightly against her body, and pulled it snug, and she was trussed helplessly. She jerked spasmodically back and forth for a moment, sobbing in desperation. Finally she quit struggling and lay back, panting heavily.

"I wouldn't have pulled you off that horse if I'd known you were a girl," he said.

"You were waiting for me," she said.

"No," he said. "I was just taking a ride to Carlsbad."

"You were waiting for me," she muttered savagely. "In those trees."

"Honest John told me someone took a pot shot at him the other day off Jacarilla Ridge," he said. "I thought maybe they'd be back. What have you got against John?"

She began to struggle again. "I didn't know who it was. They were after me. They're all after me. It seems I've been running all my life. I wasn't even safe in town. They think I know. Well, maybe I do. They'll find out. Dad knew. That's why they killed him."

She began struggling again and crying with frustrated rage. He hunkered down, grabbing her by the shoulder. Her long black hair was matted and full of thorns and burrs, and her young face was smudged and dirty. With his hand on her that way, he realized how painfully thin she was. Her struggles had become more violent, and she was crying hysterically now.

"Go ahead and kill me. That's what you're here for, aren't you? You're one of them? Go ahead. . . ."

His hand made a sharp crack against her face, jerking her head to one side. It stopped her. She quit crying and jerking around and lay there, trembling, staring up at him with wide blue eyes.

"I didn't come to kill you," he said, and bent closer, brushing her hair off one side of her face. "Aren't you Edward Alden's girl?"

Her eyes were on his right shoulder, and she must have realized it for the first time. "The one-armed man," she said, and her head turned back so she could stare up at his face. "Bob Tulare!"

"That's right," he said, and began untying her. "I thought I remembered you. Must be a year since I worked those Flying W bronc's for your dad. You've changed."

"I'm eighteen," she said, sitting up with his help. "Old enough to find who killed Dad and kill them for it."

"I thought he committed suicide when he went bankrupt," said Tulare.

She shook her head, brushing dirt out of her hair, and rubbed a torn place in her flannel shirt. "Dad was found at his desk with a bullet through his brain. I'll never believe he killed himself. He wasn't that kind. Just the night before he talked with me all evening about his plans for moving farther West and building again. He was all enthused, even drawing up the plans for the house."

She was speaking swiftly, something ineffably wild in the little jerks of her head, her eyes taking on that wary, mistrustful light as they watched him.

"Who's trying to kill you?" he asked.

She shrugged, lips thin. "I couldn't name them. After Dad was killed, my aunt took me in at Carlsbad. Even then I had begun to try and find who killed Dad, and why. I guess they thought I was getting too nosey, or too near. An attempt was made on my life. They missed me and killed my aunt. I have no one else out here, and the court tried to send me to relatives back East. I got away."

"Your father died almost a year ago," he said incredulously. "You mean you've been running around out here ever since?"

"I'll find who killed my father. . . ." She drew away suddenly, something crossing her face.

He reached out and touched her, feeling her stiffen beneath his fingers. "You've got to trust someone, Corsica."

She sat rigid, searching his face. "You were only at our spread a week, Tulare, but I liked you then. Yet . . . how can I . . . ?"

"By telling me what you've found out that made them want to kill you."

The suspicion crossed her face again. "What's your iron in this?"

"Maybe I liked you, too, that week I was there," he said. "Maybe I want to help you."

She was watching him narrowly, and she took a deep, tired breath. "Busting bronc's, you get around a bit."

"A bit."

"Maybe you know some things, too."

"How about a swap?" he said.

"You first?"

He shrugged. "Just what I've picked up here and there. Mainly how it all seems to make a pattern. Who was the first man to go bankrupt in this pasture? Must've been ten years ago. Terwilliger, or something. The Single Bar. A big outfit with a lot of cows that started disappearing just like they did for Pierce here. A few at a time. Nothing anybody could follow. Trail always cold when it was found. Must have driven Terwilliger loco, just like it's doing Pierce. Then one day Terwilliger woke up to the fact that he didn't have enough cows left on his spread to fill a corral with. So what happens? Not the usual way a cattle outfit goes when it folds. Most spreads are so heavily mortgaged that the bank gets control when they go under. But the bank was only a minor creditor in Terwilliger's case. And his other creditors took out a bankruptcy petition."

"That's the way Dad's went," she said dismally. "The last thing in his mind was bankruptcy. A cattleman just doesn't figure that way. He considers the possibility of a forced sellout or a foreclosure. But when Dad found out he'd lost too many cattle to operate any longer, it wasn't the bank that took him over. It was the receivers."

Tulare nodded. "There's your pattern. They've all gone that way. Bled dry till they can't keep going and caught in such a position that they either have to declare bankruptcy or have it filed against them. That's just one thing you won't find in the usual rustling set-up. Another is the cows themselves. What happens to them? Count up all the spreads that went the way Terwilliger and your dad did. Must be over a dozen in the past few years. That runs into thousands of cows. If they'd blotted the brands on that many critters, some brand inspector would run into it sooner or later. Yet not one has been reported."

"Did it ever occur to you that they might not change the brands?"

"That doesn't stack up," he said. "How many cattle did your father lose?"

"Around seventeen hundred," said Corsica. "We had two thousand to begin with. After the rustlers finished bleeding us, all the courts could find was three hundred."

"Try to get rid of seventeen hundred cows, known to be wet with the same brand on them you rustled them under," said Tulare. "It couldn't be done, below the border or above. Look at it from any angle, and you find your kak cinched hind side before. That's about all I know. How about what you got in your sougan?"

"I had no idea what happened to Dad was the same thing that happened to so many others," she said. "I knew several operators had declared bankruptcy lately, and I thought that was sort of odd, but not like that. I haven't much to add. I guess they tried to get rid of me more because of what they were afraid I would find out rather than what I really found. Dad had been petitioning Washington for authority to put a marshal on this case. Maybe that's why they killed him. I know Dad tracked a bunch of our rustled stock half a dozen times before, but when he found the sign, it was usually two or three days old. Mostly it led to the Pecos, and we couldn't follow it any farther than the water, or find where it came out. But once Honest John and I followed a cold trail to Jacarilla Ridge here. . . ."

"Honest John?"

She looked up at the tone of his voice. "Yes, you remember John was with us. He was the last to leave after Dad was killed. He even took me to my aunt's in town and stayed around Carlsbad several days to see I was all right. It was John who saved my life when they shot at me. He knocked me down to the sidewalk. He tried to help my aunt, too, but she had already been hit. . . ."

"But you were potting at John yesterday."

"I didn't know it was him," said Corsica. "I thought it was whoever had tried to kill me in Carlsbad. Like I said, once John and I followed the trail of some rustled stock down here. It ended in nothing, the way all the others had. But when I heard Pierce's Double Shank was beginning to have trouble with rustlers, instead of trying to find their trail, I came here to the ridge and waited. I must have been here a week before I saw the dust rising on the yonder side. I topped the ridge and saw a bunch of cattle being choused up Walnut Cañon. By the time I reached the cañon proper, they had disappeared completely. There's a lot of talus over there, and I couldn't even find any decent tracks."

"Big bunch?"

"Fifty head, maybe."

"What's at the other end of Walnut Cañon?"

"It cuts through that mesa country to a bunch of badlands on the other side. I almost got lost in there several times hunting for the trail."

"Your horse won't have run far," said Tulare. "How about showing me the cañon?"

She shrugged, and started to rise. He helped her up, feeling again all the taut, suspicious wildness in her drawn body. No wonder, he thought, running alone out here for so long, living no better than an animal. She was dirty and painfully thin, and her pants and shirt were old and tattered, and there was no beauty in her, but somehow, holding her arm that way, he felt some dim emotion begin to stir down inside him and realized it had been a long time since he had felt that way. He let her mount the saddle and then fought the snuffy little pony around a while before he could get on its rump behind the cantle. They flanked the ridge till they found her big, gaunted gelding grazing the crop seed.

The girl lifted her horse over the ridge in a tireless trot that made Tulare realize it must have been a good animal once. His own pony had to keep a canter to match the pace, and they dropped down through slippery talus and trailed hesitantly through a spread of horseweed into the badlands westward of Jacarilla Ridge. Brooding Spanish dagger was silhouetted against the sky, standing atop the mesas flanking Walnut Cañon, and the sound of their horses over talus was echoed mournfully back and forth from the rising walls of sandstone. Corsica Alden showed Tulare where she had trailed the cattle in, and lost them. He got down, hunting for sign across the talus. There were scratches across the shale that might have meant something, and spots where the rock had sloughed off under hoofed feet, but it led in no definite direction, and farther westward all sign ceased.

"Looks like they were milling around here a lot," he said, poking at the rocks with his boot. "I don't see. . . ."

It was the flapping sound that stopped him. He whirled toward the wall of sandstone towering behind him, striking blindly at the fluttering, clawing thing descending on his head. He heard the girl cry out sharply, and he seemed surrounded by the flapping black madness. Flailing with his arm, he stumbled backward, blinded; he tripped over a rock, and went flat on his back.

"Tulare!" called the girl. "Tulare, what is it?"

Lying down that way, he was free of them, and he could see what it was. "Get down, Corsica, lie down. Let them pass over you. It's a bunch of bats."

By the time she got down, they were gone anyway, flapping out into the night. Tulare rose, rubbing his eye where one had struck him, bending to peer at the sandstone. He could hear Corsica, breathing heavily behind him.

"Must be a crack somewhere here," he said, pulling at the loose strata.

"Oh, don't." Her voice was strained. "You're liable to let out some more of those horrible things."

The sandstone crumbled away beneath his fingers, and he found the crevice, hidden behind some ocotillo. Another bat flapped out, and Corsica gave a little cry. Tulare kept digging till he had uncovered a nook that kept widening as the sandstone crumbled.

"Must be some sort of a cave. . . ."

"I imagine," said a lazy voice from somewhere behind them, "and, if you dig it out a little more, it'll be just about big enough to stuff your carcasses in."

IV

Carlsbad wasn't much of a town. Sometime sat there on his fat, yawning pinto, scratching his beard and looking down on the scattering of frame buildings and thinking that. *Carlsbad wasn't much of a town.* He hadn't ever liked towns a lot, anyway. Sometime. Too much work in them. It caused him pain even to think of it. Work. He grimaced and turned to spit tobacco juice at the horsefly that had the temerity to alight on his pinto's neck.

He was a lanky man, Sometime, six feet and some when he stood straight, which nobody had ever seen him do, his bony shoulders stooped to the warmth of the hot sun, his spade beard shot with gray. His single gallus supported a pair of patched jeans, and there was an ancient over-and-under gun stuck, naked, beneath his left stirrup leather and held there by tie-thongs around its barrel and butt. He squinted his eyes now to see the horsebacker coming out of town and taking the road that would lead him to where Sometime sat his pinto there on the rise. Duval? Sometime scratched himself through the red flannels that sufficed for his shirt. Who else rode such a horse, rolling in tallow that way, and wore a tail coat with satin lapels and had such a big diamond on his finger? Sometime could catch its flash in the sun from here. Nobody else. Nobody else in Carlsbad. There were enough rich men here. But none of them advertised it the way Duval did.

"Marquette?" said Sometime.

The man had almost passed by, and he hauled his fat bay up sharply, silver-mounted rig popping as he jerked it around toward Sometime. He was a heavy, dark man, Marquette Duval, and the sweat gleamed on his forehead beneath the flat-topped black hat he wore. He sat his horse solidly with his stirrups flapped out wide and his weight thrown back farther than a cowman would want.

"I thought I told you at my house," said Duval irritably, reining his bay toward Sometime where he sat the pinto between two rocks to one side of the road. "This is too close to town."

"Your house is too far," said Sometime. "I was passing this way. Thought I might catch you coming out."

"I never was able to decide which is the laziest, you or your pinto," said Duval. His black eyes held a calculating glow. "What's up?"

"We got another bunch of Double Shank steers the other day," said Sometime. "I saw Lonoke in town today. He said he'd come in with Albert Pierce. Is this it?"

Duval shrugged. "Just about it. You've bled the Double Shank till Pierce is in the red. Eddy County is getting known as a poor risk, what with this string of bankruptcies, and Pierce can't get any backing from the East. His creditors are threatening to take out a bankruptcy petition against him. That's what he was in town for today. With the aid of the courts, he managed to hold the creditors off another couple of weeks."

"Why should the courts do that? They got something in the saddle?"

Duval brushed a finger absently across his clipped mustache. "I don't know. Might have a man looking around."

"I thought you spiked that petition Alden sent to Washington for a marshal."

"I did," said Duval. "The federal government claimed they had no jurisdiction over it till one of the rustled beeves was found outside the county. And that hasn't happened yet. But this wouldn't have to be a federal officer. Any investigator they have out is more liable to be working through the sheriff's office, since it's still up to the county. Or maybe Pierce hired a private dick of his own."

"There's a new bronc'-buster out at the Double Shank."

Duval shrugged. "You know who that is. Bob Tulare. Where are you going to find any investigator, county, state, federal or otherwise, who can bust bronc's like that one-armed redhead does? It takes a lifetime of flash-riding to get that good. A lawman just wouldn't have the time to be that good on the bronc's."

"Lonoke doesn't agree with you," said Sometime. "Lonoke told me he tried to stop Tulare from the beginning because he figured the redhead was something besides a bronc'-peeler. Lonoke even gave the one-armed scratcher that pied killer nobody's been able to break. It didn't discourage Tulare none."

Duval tilted his head, pursing his lips. "I'll see what I can find out about him, then."

"You do that." Sometime stopped to consider something, then narrowed his eyes at the other man. "Duval, we been thinking."

"Is it possible?"

No expression showed on Sometime's long face. "When Edward Alden declared bankruptcy and the courts took over his Flying W last year, you told us Alden's books showed that he originally ran eighteen hundred head of cattle before we began to bleed his outfit."

"That's right," said Duval. "Eighteen hundred. You relieved him of fifteen hundred. That left three hundred the courts rounded up."

"I've been seeing a lot of Clarence Peters lately," said Sometime. "Peters ramrodded that roundup for the courts on Alden's Flying W. Last week I got him drunk enough to spill some beans. He saw Alden's books, and he says they tallied two thousand steers originally."

Duval's saddle creaked beneath his shifting weight. "Did it ever occur to you that there might have been a miscount?"

"On whose side?" asked Sometime. "The courts got paid for three hundred Flying W steers. We got paid on fifteen hundred. If the original tally was two thousand, that leaves two hundred steers somebody sold and got paid for without letting either the courts or us know. At ten dollars a head, that many cows would buy a mighty nice saddle for a man. That a new saddle you're forking?"

Duval flushed. "I showed you the check stubs from the Kansas City bank. Paid on eighteen hundred steers."

Sometime scratched himself through his red flannels. "If you can juggle those checks on the courts, you can juggle them on us just as well. Before we touch another of Pierce's Double Shank steers, Duval, we'd like our share of what you got off those extra two hundred Flying W cows last year."

Duval's bay jerked up with his vicious pull on the reins. "I only got paid for eighteen hundred steers. I don't like your insinuations."

"Insinuations?" It was the first time Sometime had grinned. It was slow and lazy, revealing tobacco-stained teeth. "I'm not insinuating, Duval, I'm telling you right out."

Duval necked his horse with a jerk, and the bay side-stepped against Sometime's pinto, almost knocking it over. Duval's dark face was mottled with diffused blood, and he gripped his big Mexican horn with one white-knuckled hand, speaking through his teeth.

"I won't take it, Sometime. You can't accuse me like that. We've been working together too long now. I've never dealt you one card off the bottom. . . ."

"You mean we never caught you dealing from there before," said Sometime. "How many other times did you hold out a stub on us as well as on the courts, Duval?"

Duval stiffened in his saddle, then he jerked his hand off the horn and fully slapped Sometime in the face. It knocked Sometime sidewise on his pinto, but he caught at Duval's hand before the man could pull it back, keeping himself from falling that way. He straightened up, yanking Duval toward him by the hand, then, grabbing Duval's coat, he held the man bent painfully out of his saddle, and their faces were not an inch apart.

"You shouldn't have done that, Duval," said Sometime, and his voice held that lazy drawl.

"Let me go, Sometime," gasped Duval, trying to jerk away. "I swear, I'll kill you."

"Will you?" said Sometime.

"Let me go," screamed Duval, and twisted in Sometime's grasp to grab beneath his fustian. Sometime knew what that meant, and his own move seemed languorous beside Duval's violent jerks. He released his hold on Duval's coat and bent down between their horses with a weary grunt. It was a Belgian pepperbox Duval got out, with four ugly Damascus barrels. But before he could line it up, Sometime had caught the man's foot, pulling it from the stirrup and heaving upward almost lazily. Duval's gun went off into the air as he fell off the other side of his saddle. He caught wildly at the horn, but his weight was already off, and the bay spooked to one side, and Duval fell on his back to the ground. Crying with his rage, he rolled over on his belly and grabbed for the Belgian gun he had dropped.

"When you pick it up," said Sometime, "take it by the barrel and toss it toward that cactus over there."

Duval stiffened, his hand stretched out toward the pepperbox. Then, without rolling back over, he twisted his white face around so he could see Sometime. The tall man sat his yawning pinto with one knee hooked up over the slick horn, the over-and-under gun resting across his hip and pointing in the general direction of Duval. For a long moment Duval lay there, rigid, staring at Sometime. Then, spasmodically, he took the Belgian gun by its steel barrels and threw it toward the spread of cactus some ten feet away.

"That's the smart dogie, Duval. And the next time I see you, I want what you owe us on that two hundred head of Flying W steers. And if you have any ideas about reaching that cutter of yours and unraveling some lead while my back is turned, riding away . . ."—Sometime patted his over-and-under—"you might as well tell me right now which you'd like through your brisket, the Thirty-Thirty slug I got in the top of this cannon, or the load of sixteen gauge I got in the bottom."

Somewhere a hoot owl mourned at the moon. The shale rattled eerily beneath the pinto's feet. Sometime nodded sleepily in the saddle, free-bitting his horse because it knew the way well enough. Jacarilla Ridge was behind him, and the walls of Walnut Cañon were lit bizarrely on either side by the moon. It had been a long ride from Carlsbad, and the last ten miles had been the worst, working through the badlands between Jacarilla Ridge and this cañon.

At first, as he wended his way down the narrowing cañon, he thought it was the bats. They always came out at night. Then he realized it was something more. He put a little pressure on the bit, and the paint stopped, yawning.

"Tulare," called someone from ahead. "Tulare, what is it?"

Tulare? Sometime sat a little straighter in his saddle, scratching himself through his red flannels. He contemplated the ground for a while, then shook his head. He could get close enough on his horse without them hearing him, and the bats would cover what sound he made after that anyway. One of the bats flapped past him higher up as he gigged the pinto on forward, bending to untie the saddle thongs from around his over-and-under gun. A turn in the cañon showed the two horses up ahead, and, a little beyond that, two people. Sometime let his pinto walk in past the ground-hitched mounts. The girl and man were turned toward the sandstone, and the man was digging with his hands.

"Must be some sort of a cave," he said.

"I imagine," put in Sometime, "and if you dig it out a little more, it'll be just about big enough to stuff your carcasses in."

The man turned, moving his hand as he did. Then his hand stopped, far enough away from the iron grips of his big Remington, and his eyes rested for that moment on Sometime's gun. Sometime took in his reddish complexion and thought maybe he would be a blond without that flat-topped hat on, and then saw his right shoulder.

"Well, Wingy," said Sometime, "you're a long way from home."

"You herd the bats?" said the man.

Sometime waved his gun toward the girl. "She called you Tulare? Maybe you were hunting for something special."

"Strays," said Tulare.

"In here?" Sometime cheeked his tobacco to spit. Then he looked at them quizzically. "I don't think so. You get on your horses, and we'll take a *pasear*."

The pinto yawned, and Sometimes yawned, watching them mount. Then he waved them ahead of him, and followed them down the cañon. Small caves began to pock the walls now, and once in a while a bat flapped by. They were riding on a granite shelf that left no marks behind, and Sometime grinned at the thought of anybody trying to trail anything in here. Strays? No. Tulare?

Finally he stopped them before one of the caves, drawing his pinto in close to the one-armed man. "Light down."

There was something tense and waiting about Tulare's lean body, dismounting. Sometime didn't like the wild look to the girl, either. It had come to him now. Corsica Alden. He hadn't recognized her at first; she was so thin and drawn-looking. He told Tulare to turn around. Then he reached out with the tip of his over-and-under gun, catching Tulare's Remington beneath its butt and lifting it out of the holster and dropping it to the ground. He moved them ahead and got the Remington off the ground and stuck it in the waistband of his trousers. He took up the reins of the two horses of the intruders and motioned with his gun.

The girl stared at the dark mouth of the cave. "In there?"

"Unless you'd rather stay out here with a load of buckshot in your liver," said Sometime.

He saw the way Corsica caught at Tulare's hand as they stepped into the cave, and wondered how long they had been like that. Or maybe it was the caves. It always affected you like that at first. He fumbled around just inside for the buckthorn torch and found it finally thrust into a niche. He lit the *entraña,* and its flaring light threw their shadows, huge and grotesque, across the descending floor of the cave. As they moved on in, the ceiling grew in height. The pinto plodded stolidly after Sometime, accustomed to the hollow echoes their every movement made, but the other horses kept spooking and shying. Then the light from the *entraña* fell across the first stalactite, pendant from the roof, a greenish, translucent hue, and the weird unearthly beauty of it stopped Tulare and Corsica for a moment.

"Move your hocks," said Sometime. "You'll see everything."

His voice boomed hollowly through the cavern. Corsica turned toward him jerkily, then moved on. The horses began to yank back as the first dripping of the water reached them. Sometime pulled them on, passing the water seeping from the roof above to fall on the stalagmite that had been forming through the ages on the floor. Farther on a stalagmite and stalactite had met, forming a column. Sometime saw Tulare keep looking at the floor, and knew what he had seen. He shrugged. It didn't matter now. Tulare wouldn't get back out to tell. Reaching the first spot where the cave branched, Sometime lifted his torch to find the chink he had cut out with an axe to tell him which branch to take. The acoustics magnified every sound so much that he could even hear Tulare's breathing begin to get faster, and he pulled the gun back a little farther in the crook of his elbow and got a tighter grip on the horses. *Go ahead and try it,* he thought, *if you got the hankering.* The roof lowered ahead abruptly, and the trail wound through a low rock-cut passage where the gypsum crystals formed sparkling bunches of grapes on the roof. One of the horses stumbled, and Sometime saw Tulare's shoulders stiffen, and then relax. Sometime had the reins of the horses around the elbow of the arm that held the torch, and the constant tug and jerk of the two spooky mounts caused the light to waver uncertainly across the floor. Maybe that was why the girl didn't see how the trail was formed ahead. It made a sharp-angle turn into a wall of rock that rose out of sight on one side, the other side of the trail dropping off into a pit that had never been plumbed. Sometime was about to warn them when the girl tripped and stumbled, plunging head first toward the edge of the trail. Tulare had her arm, and he was yanked forward, too.

"Corsica!" he shouted, and his voice was magnified a thousand times into a gargantuan roar whose echoes slapped back and forth through the caverns, sending the horses into a veritable frenzy. The torch was jerked out of Sometime's hand, bouncing across the limestone and falling over the lip of the trail, its light casting a last dim glow that silhouetted the rocky edge, then extinguishing abruptly. The utter darkness was filled with the screaming of the spooked horses, and their plunging, wheeling movement, and Sometime heard Tulare shout something up ahead. He was groping for the wall when he sensed someone in front of him.

"Tulare?" he called. "Tulare, don't start anything. I'll let you have this buckshot. Tulare . . . !"

He heard the movement, and his fingers closed over the trigger spasmodically. The gunshot drowned all other sound in that instant, and then the terrible thunderous echoes of it swept back and forth, hurting Sometime's ears so much he cried out with the pain. The body hurtling into him knocked him back against the wall, and he felt that one hand clawing at the Remington he had stuffed in his waist, and he knew who it was. Sometime levered his over-and-under gun between them across Tulare's body, shoving the man backward, slashing downward with it to knock Tulare's hand off the butt of the Remington. With that much room between them, Sometime gave a last heave with the levered gun to knock Tulare backward, and then jerked it around and squeezed the trigger. This time it was the .30-30 slug in the upper barrel, and even with the *boom* of the shot he heard Tulare scream. Then it was the echoes, dying reluctantly in the womb of the cavern somewhere, and then it was nothing. Sometime shoved his gun out in front of him, feeling around on the narrow trail with the end of the barrel. He could reach the edge of the trail without moving from where he stood.

"Tulare?" It was Corsica Alden's voice, surprisingly close. "Tulare, was that you? What happened?"

Sometime fished a match from the pocket of his jeans, and its flare revealed the girl standing back against the wall on the other side of the trail, hands spread out against the limestone. She looked at Sometime, his long face eerily lit in the flickering light, and then her eyes passed him, and he saw the realization in them, and the horror. He followed her gaze over the edge of the trail into the bottomless murk.

"That's what happened," he said.

V

The noise had spooked his horse, and Honest John stood there beside the animal, holding its head down and stroking its neck, peering toward the mouth of the cave. There was no more sound from inside the cave, and, when the horse had quieted, he hitched the reins to some Spanish dagger and slipped his boots off, hooking a thumb through the straps to carry them. Then he got his ancient brass-framed Prescott Navy from its holster and moved in. The way they had been shooting, it looked like a real corpse and cartridge occasion. His feet slid over the limestone without much sound, and then, abruptly, from ahead he heard the clatter of a running horse and threw himself back against the rough wall. The animal charged by him wildly, reins flapping free, and galloped on into the open.

Finally John began moving on in. It was utter darkness

now, and silence for a long time, and, when sound came again, it wasn't shots, or voices. It was a small scratching, rustling sound, intensified now, ceasing for a moment, then starting up again. Finally he reached the spot where it seemed to emanate from, and stood there, head cocked to one side. From below? He waited a while longer before he spoke.

"You got an itch?" he said, and moved aside from where he had stood.

The answer didn't come for a while, and then someone spoke, muffled and distant. "Who is it? Sometime?"

"Anytime," said Honest John. "Anytime at all. Where are you?"

"Over the edge of the trail. Hit a ledge down here or something."

John lit a match and threw it out in front of him so he would be out of the light. It struck the floor and flamed there a moment, and no shots came. After it had gone out, he felt his way to the edge of the limestone and lit another match; this time he dropped it over the lip of the rock and peered down. Its falling light momentarily revealed the figure crouched on the ledge far below, taut face strained upwards. Then the match fell on into the bottomless void, and the light went out.

"I got my horse outside," said Honest John. "I'll get my dally and see if we can't pull you out."

It took him a long time to go back out of the cave and get his rope off the horse. This was what he got for taking a hankering to that one-armed boy. This was just what he got. Maybe Forty-Rod was right. He was a damned sentimentalist. Mind his own business and he wouldn't have all this trouble. He should really leave Tulare down there. That would be the smart thing. Just leave him down there to rot. He had reached the right section of the cave floor by that time, and he began to chip two deep grooves out of the limestone with his Barlow knife. Then he put his boots back on and dropped the uncoiled dally over the edge of the trail. He was a damned old fool, that's all.

"Any reason you can't climb this clothesline?"

"No," said Tulare from below. "Nothing broken."

"Let me get set then. I'll holler when you can begin."

Honest John snubbed his end of the rope around his waist and moved back against the wall, planting his high boot heels into the two holes he had dug in the limestone, leaning backward. Then he called, and felt the tug of the rope, and it had begun. At times his little old body was almost pulled over by the jerking, twitching, pulling weight of Tulare coming up, and the sweat was soggy under his armpits and down his back, and he was breathing like a *soldado*'s horse. Finally he heard the scrape of Tulare's body over the rim of the ledge, and he gave a final yank on the rope and moved over to grab the one-armed man.

"Thanks," gasped Tulare. "Honest John? Thanks. I was going backward when Sometime let me have that second load. It went over my head, I guess, and I couldn't stop myself falling. Thought I'd busted my back when I hit that ledge."

"Sometime?" said Honest John. "That's what you meant. He was here?"

"Here!" Tulare was on his feet now, and his voice had a hoarse, driven sound. "He's got the girl. He's mixed in with the rustlers somehow, John."

"Oh, now, don't make me eat them *frijoles*," said Honest John. "Not Sometime. He's too lazy to even look at a cow, much less to rustle it. He's just an old crow-bait, boy. He's been around these parts so long I'm surprised he hasn't taken root."

181

"He's mixed up with the rustlers, I tell you," panted Tulare. "I saw sign coming through the cave, John. Cow sign. Droppings and hoof prints in the soft part and hair caught along the walls. And he's got the girl."

"Girl?"

"Corsica Alden."

"Now I know that fall clabbered your brains, boy. Corsica Alden's been dead over a year. She disappeared from Carlsbad right after her father's death. You must know that."

"No." Tulare's boots made a sudden shuffle on the limestone. "She's here, John. I'm getting her. Sometime's got her in this cave somewhere, and I'm getting her."

"Don't be a fool," said Honest John. "Even if she is here, you couldn't find her now. Go any farther into this cave and you'll lose yourself as well as the girl. There's one branch back of us we passed already. The only reason I didn't take the wrong turn is I was following the sounds you made. There must be other branches farther on. Hundreds of them. Get twisted up in here and you'll never get out. If you want to find anybody, you'll have to get help. Let's go back to the Double Shank and get some of the boys and a lot of twine and some bull's-eye lanterns."

"And leave her here?" Tulare tried to tear his arm out of the old man's grip. "No, I'm going to find her, John. I've got to. We can't leave her like this."

"You wouldn't help her any by getting lost yourself."

Tulare tore loose, and John realized it was the only way, now. He took a jump after the younger man, catching him by the arm with one hand, and pushed his gun's barrel into the small of Tulare's back.

Tulare stopped, with the feel of it in his back, and John's voice had suddenly taken on a thin edge. "Now, unless you want me to send you to hell on a shutter, just turn around and march out of this cave in front of me."

Tulare stood rigidly, and it was a long moment before he spoke, and it finally came in a hoarse, strained way. "You sound like you mean it."

John shoved his gun a little harder against Tulare's back. "Maybe you think I don't."

They were handling the bronchos in the main corral of the Double Shank when Tulare and Honest John got back. Lonoke was on a bay Tulare had broken the other day, trotting it around the fence and changing its lead every few feet. He stopped it by the gate as Honest John dismounted there.

"Looks like it might make a good cutting horse," said Honest John, nodding at the bay. "How does it neck?"

"Where the hell have you been?" Lonoke asked Tulare angrily. "We haven't been able to do anything but work those bronc's you scratched yesterday. I want the rest of them finished today."

Tulare's horse hadn't run far from the cave, and he and Honest John had found it wandering toward the Double Shank near the end of Walnut Cañon. Without getting off, Tulare told Lonoke about Sometime and Corsica.

"Sometime?" laughed Lonoke. "Where did you get your red-eye? Sometime wouldn't have the energy to look at a wet cow. I think you went to town and got drunk."

Honest John shook his head. "There might be something in what he says, Lonoke. I heard some shooting and such going on before I reached him."

"What were you doing in Walnut Cañon, anyway?" Lonoke asked John.

"When Tulare left the Double Shank last night," said Honest John, "I remembered how you thought he'd come here for something more than bronc'-busting when he first showed, and I thought it was sort of late to be heading to Carlsbad, so I follered him. I lost him somewhere over by Jacarilla Ridge. Come morning, I was topping the ridge and saw a rider heading up Walnut Cañon. I guess it was Sometime. At the time, though, I thought it was Tulare, and I follered him in. I would have lost them all if I hadn't heard that shooting from the cave."

"Are you going to help me find that girl?" asked Tulare. "Talk here won't get her out. Honest John said there were some spools of twine up at the big house. I'll go get them from Pierce. We'll need some lanterns and plenty of dally ropes. You round up your crew, Lonoke, and I'll meet you here in fifteen minutes."

"Look who's giving orders," said Lonoke.

"Maybe he *should* give the orders," said Forty-Rod Farnum. "You won't be giving them much longer."

They all turned to where the fat man sat his enormous mare behind Tulare. Honest John had been too intent on the other men to notice Forty-Rod ride up.

"What did you say?" snapped Lonoke.

"I said you won't be giving orders much longer," Forty-Rod told him. "Your tenure of office is reaching its termination, Lonoke. Another transaction or two such as the one which has just occurred, and there won't be any Double Shank for you to ramrod."

"Transaction like what?" said Lonoke angrily. "Will you wipe the mud off your saddle."

"If you mean my methods of expression are obscure to you, I can't remedy that," said Forty-Rod ponderously. "To put it succinctly, another bunch of cattle has been extirpated from your rapidly diminishing north herd."

"That's right," said Henry Desha, sitting his lathered horse beside Forty-Rod. "Another bunch of steers was cut out. Don't know exactly when. Time we found out, the trail was cold."

Lonoke turned slowly in his saddle till he was looking at Tulare. "So you saw cow sign in the caves."

"Now, let's not jump to conclusions," said Forty-Rod.

"I'm not jumping to any conclusions," said Lonoke hotly. "They're already here. Damn' right Tulare saw cow sign in the caves. He probably got knocked off onto that ledge by the cows he was running in there."

"Don't be a damn' fool, Lonoke," said Tulare. "How could I have rustled your cattle? If you aren't going to help me get that girl, I'll do it alone. I'm not wasting any more time around this here horse hole."

"You're not going anywhere." Lonoke stepped out of his saddle onto the fence, ducking through. "Desha, get him!"

Tulare had necked his horse to get it out from between the fence and the head of Forty-Rod's mare, but Desha jabbed his own lathered mount with his gut hooks, jumping it ahead to cut off Tulare. Lonoke reached Tulare from the inside, grabbing at his leg. Tulare kicked him in the face and raked his mount with his other spur. The hairy little pony leaped under the rowel, but Desha's big dun was in front of it now, and the two of them made a fleshy thud, meeting. Forty-Rod's big mare reared up over the other two horses, and the gross man rolled backward out of the saddle, shouting fulminations. Honest John tried to grab Desha's bridle and jerk his dun out of Tulare's way, but Desha had sidled in and caught Tulare, and the two of them were grappling. Lonoke came up behind Honest John, grabbing at Tulare again just as Desha's dun side-stepped, shoving Tulare's black pony over into the fence and pinning both Lonoke and John.

Lonoke went down beneath the horse's hoofs, trying to get out from between the fence and the black, and John was shouting with the agony of all that weight against him. Tulare stood in his stirrups, grappling with Desha, and Desha was pulled far out to one side off his dun. The black pony plunged forward suddenly, its hairy shoulders smashing into a corral post and cracking it. That section of the fence gave suddenly, and John fell backward through the wrecked bars. The black pony plunged forward again, trying to get out from between the smashed fence and the dun, and Tulare was thrown over its rump, pulling Desha with him. The two men fell into the tilted wreckage of the fence, bars cracking beneath them as they rolled across, and then fell on into the corral, still struggling.

The dun and the black were away now, and Lonoke was getting to his feet, face bloody. Cursing bitterly, he jumped up the tilted fence and dropped off the broken top bar onto Desha and Tulare. John got up groggily, his chest hurting, and turned to get into the corral the same way Lonoke had. Forty-Rod had regained his feet, and he grabbed at Honest John.

"Don't be a fool. You'll only cause us more trouble by interfering."

Desha grunted sickly as Tulare hit him in the face, and Honest John tore free of Forty-Rod. "You gonna let them do that to the boy?"

"Oh, very well," grumbled Forty-Rod, grabbing the tilting fence to climb in after Honest John. "I always did think Lonoke was a lentiginose excrement anyway."

John was just about to jump on the writhing men below the tilting fence when he saw it. Kensington had been over by the chute with another Double Shank hand, getting a broncho in from the larger corral, but, seeing the fight, both men had started this way on the run.

"Kensington!" shouted John. "Don't. You forgot the

chute. You got that killer in there. Go back and close the chute . . . !"

John was cut off by Forty-Rod's shoving at him from behind, and the two of them crashed off the fence into Desha and Lonoke and Tulare. Desha had risen to his knees above Lonoke and the one-armed man, and was yanking out his gun to pistol-whip Tulare. Honest John got his skinny arms about Desha's thick neck and yanked him back off balance, and both of them rolled away from the others. Desha tore Honest John's arms loose with a curse.

"Get out of here before I hurt you, old man!" he shouted hoarsely.

"Old man, is it?" Honest John scrambled to his feet, whipping out his own gun and throwing himself at Desha. Desha tried to bring his weapon up and catch John on the side of the head, but John knocked the gun aside with his own big Prescott. Then he caught Desha with a vicious sideways kick that knocked both feet out from under the stubby man, and, as Desha went down, John hit him viciously back of the neck with the gun, and Desha stayed on the ground where he fell. "Old man, is it?"

"Misbegotten son of Satan's unsanctified lubricity," grunted Forty-Rod, and he had hauled Lonoke off Tulare with both hands on Lonoke's collar, pulling him erect, and then releasing him and hitting him in the face with a fist that would have felled the biggest Black Angus bull that ever waded in bluegrass. Kensington and the other Double Shanker jumped Tulare before he could rise, and the one-armed man threw himself against them on his knees, hugging at their legs with his one arm to keep them from kicking him. Honest John got around behind Kensington and caught his arm as the man swung it back to slug Tulare; he hooked it upward in a hammerlock, striking at Kensington's head with his

187

pistol barrel. Kensington shouted with the pain, jerking backward groggily. He twisted aside to avoid John's next blow and pulled out of the hammerlock, turning on John with a haymaker that caught the older man on the button.

In the bright flash of pain, John felt himself staggering back toward the center of the corral, and then the hard-packed turf was gritty against his back. He saw Kensington come down on top of him with both boots, and all the air went out of him as the heels dug into his belly. He caught at Kensington's legs, pulling the man down so he could strike with the Prescott again. Sprawled out on top of John, Kensington caught the brass-framed revolver and twisted it from the old man's hands. Nauseated with pain, John rolled from beneath Kensington and tried to get to his feet, but one of his legs must have twisted beneath him when he fell, because, when he put his weight on it, the pain was too great to bear, and he fell back to his hands and knees.

He suddenly realized Kensington was no longer there, and, turning his head, he could make out the man backing toward the fence, his twisted face turned past John toward the other side of the corral.

"Get out of the corral!" Kensington shouted hoarsely. "That killer's loose. Somebody get a rope. Get out of the corral."

Maddened by being pinned in the chute, excited by the shouting, fighting men, the pied horse was whinnying shrilly and butting into the fence in an effort to get out. John had seen blind buckers like that before that got so frenzied they would run into anything in their way. Kensington's movement must have caught its bloodshot eyes, because the piebald turned away from the fence suddenly, head rising. John couldn't help his spasmodic move to get up, and again his leg caved in beneath him, and he knew it had been his mistake.

"Get that rope, Tulare!" Kensington's voice rose shrilly. "The killer's seen John. Get that rope."

John sensed the shuffling movement of the men behind him, and heard Forty-Rod shout something, and then the black gave an ugly little pump-handle buck, its front legs hitting before its hind, and broke into a charge like a Brahma bull. John made a swipe at his holster and then remembered how Kensington had tossed his gun out of reach, and he stared up at the oncoming piebald, wide-eyed, not feeling any fear, just seeing it there and knowing how it would end now.

"You can't do it with a rope this time, boy," he said.

Then, somehow, under the ground-shaking thunder of the oncoming horse, there was a lighter thud behind John, and a blurred figure went by him on the dead run. John didn't actually realize who it was till the man had reached the horse. He couldn't have done it going head-on; he had come in from the flank, so that his left arm was on the inside, running in so that his whole side struck the horse's shoulder at the same time his hand caught the saddle horn and his outside foot swung up. It was an Indian mount that maybe only one man in a thousand could have done, and Tulare did it. His hold on the horn acted as a lever against his own momentum and the horse's momentum, swinging his whole body up as soon as he kicked into the air with that outside leg and throwing himself around so he hit the saddle face forward. He didn't try to find the stirrups. Tucking his knees under the bucking roll, he jerked the reins off the horn and slid his fist down them till he had the ribbons bunched on the horse's neck, and then yanked viciously to one side. It hadn't been worked into neck-reining yet, but the cruel Spanish bit turned the horse just enough. Maybe it missed John by a foot. John choked in the dust as it thundered by him, and, when he could see again, the imprint of a hoof indented the ground right beside the hand he was supporting himself on.

The piebald had gotten the bit in its teeth now, and Tulare hadn't tried to fight it any more. Kensington and Forty-Rod and Desha scattered before the oncoming beast.

"Take a dive!" shouted Forty-Rod. "Sun your moccasins, Tulare. That horse'll never take the fence. Roll off. You'll go right into those bars . . . !"

But Tulare had bent forward over the killer, and his face contorted as he gave it a vicious rake with his gut hooks. The horse grunted, and, although it had already been charging, it seemed to shoot forward under the spurs, and Tulare gave it a full rein. For that last moment, John thought, it was going to ram the fence. Then he saw the ripple of muscle across its lathered flanks as it gathered itself, and saw the front hoofs lift, and the back hoofs, and it sailed over Lonoke where he lay just inside the wrecked portion of the fence, and its hoofs cleared the tilting top rail with feet to spare. John felt the ground shake as the horse came down outside the corral.

Tulare let it run a moment, and then began raking the beast again, and finally he gouged it into bucking. Kensington and Forty-Rod and Desha forgot Lonoke, then, and Honest John; they stood tensely on the inside of the broken fence, watching Tulare ride that killer. John crouched there on the ground, open-mouthed, his breath caught in him. The broncho started out by hiding its head and kicking off the lid, leaving the ground with all four legs stiff as pokers and coming down in a pile driver. But Tulare's body was limp when the horse struck that way, and he took the awful grinding shock without much apparent pain.

"Rake him!" shouted John. "Take that pile driver out of him. He'll knock your tailbone through your skull that way. Rake him."

Tulare did. He gave his legs a free swing and raked the piebald from shoulders to flank. The animal screamed frenziedly
under the pain of the rowels, and quit pile driving to buck
straight away. The reddish dust boiled up around its lashing
hoofs, and, when John could see clearly again, the beast was
sunfishing. It came back toward the fence, and it seemed that
it was almost touching the ground with its shoulders, first
one, then the other, twisting over so far the sun caught on its
belly. Before it could smash into the fence, Tulare curried it
again, and the horse swapped ends wildly, trying to get away
from the maddening spurs. Tulare had thrown his weight to
the inside as the killer swapped ends, and he was still tense
with that movement when the animal pulled a double-shuffle.
It threw Tulare partly off balance, and the piebald must have
sensed it, because it began sunfishing again.

Honest John saw Tulare's weight jerk to one side as the
horse twisted toward the other, and for a moment he thought
the one-armed man was going off. But Tulare had a pair of
legs like steel springs. Without grabbing the apple, he threw
himself the other way, raking the horse wildly to bring it out
of that sunfishing. There was something desperate in the way
the broncho started cloud-hunting now, and John knew he
was seeing the beginning of the end. It bucked on a dime, and
every time it hit the ground, Tulare gave it the grappling irons
again. The beast was foamy with lather, and its bucking was
getting weaker and weaker. Finally it gave a last crow hop,
and then stood there, head down, beaten.

Tulare slid off and leaned against the animal, and John
couldn't tell which was trembling the more, man or beast.
Finally Kensington and Desha came out and got the horse.
Desha was sullen about it, but Kensington hadn't known
what the fight was about anyway, and he kept slapping
Tulare on the back, grinning all over. Forty-Rod came over

and helped up Honest John.

John pointed to the hoof prints passing the spot where he had crouched. "That's the second time the boy saved my ornery hide. One more inch and I would've been hamburger."

"For once in your life, you have not uttered a prevarication," said Forty-Rod.

Kensington and Desha took the stunned, beaten piebald back into the corral and then came back to carry Lonoke to the water trough to bring him around. Forty-Rod helped John to the cook shack and began hunting for some Sloan's liniment to rub on his twisted leg.

"Listen," said John. "Can't we keep that boy from going to the caves?"

Forty-Rod shook his head sadly. "I'm really sorry Tulare had to save your misguided life. Now we will have to go through that all over again. Not enough that he had to pull you from death's mordacious jaws once. No. Twice. I told you he could engender nothing but inordinate biblioclasm for us. And now you want to keep him from visiting those alveolar excavations. You should know by now that there is only one thing which will stop that man from doing whatever he sets out to do. Of course, if you wish me to perform that function. . . ."

"No!" John's voice was sharp. "Don't you do that, Forty-Rod. I won't have it, understand. He saved my life twice. Go out and get him and bring him here. Maybe we can talk him out of it."

Shrugging gross shoulders, the fat cook waddled out of the door. It was a long time before his bulk was silhouetted again in the portal.

"I fear we will have to let the bats apprehend Tulare," said Forty-Rod. "He's gone."

192

Valley of Secret Guns

VI

The horse-maiming cactus drew its green ugliness across the harsh bare rock and thrust up malignant spines to the last, dying light of the sun dropping behind Jacarilla Ridge. The hairy black pony shifted restlessly in the dry mesquite. Squatting there with a three days' stubble turning his long chin red, Tulare squinted through the haze eastward, trying to see if it was dust now.

He had gotten some spools of twine from the big house at the Double Shank and a bull's-eye lantern, and had ridden the rest of the day back to the caves, but his search in there had been fruitless. They were a veritable mass of caverns and tunnels, and his twine had soon run out. A hundred men with all the twine in Carlsbad couldn't have begun to explore the caverns. Tulare realized there was only one way to find Corsica, if Sometime still had her in there, and if the rustlers were using the caves to hide the cattle. It was a long shot. But it was all he had left. He had spent a day hunting in the caves, and now two more days waiting up here in this niche on Jacarilla Ridge, hidden from below.

There was a small, growing excitement in him as he tried to separate the scrawl of dust from the afternoon haze. It had caught his eyes a few minutes ago, a color tawnier than the sky itself, sifting up from the basin east of the ridge. Before the sunlight faded completely, Tulare knew what it was. He crawled to his black pony and led it down a gully through the twilight until he had reached level ground. Then he mounted and headed across the ten miles of badlands to Walnut Cañon. His horse was lathered and blowing when he reached the mouth of the cañon, and he could hear the bawl of cattle in the night ahead of him. He knew he couldn't get far down the narrow way on horseback without being spotted, but he could keep up with the walking herd on foot. He hitched his black pony to a bunch of ocotillo and worked up the north slope so he would be traveling parallel to the bunch of cattle, but above them. He was skirting some cane cactus when he heard them rattle, and whirled to see the shadowy figure jumping at him.

Tulare threw himself backward, away from the rush. The man couldn't stop himself, and he ran square into one of Tulare's knees, the air knocked out of him with a gasp. Tulare rolled over and caught at the man's legs, bringing the doubled-over body down on top of him. He caught at an arm with his hand, jerking the man over and rolling on top of him. With his free fist, the man flailed at Tulare's face, but Tulare blocked the blow with a shoulder, releasing his grip on the other arm to yank his gun. He had it snapped back to clout the man, and that way his one-armed torso must have been faintly silhouetted against the night sky.

"Tulare," panted the man, and Tulare recognized the hoarse, thick voice.

He reversed the gun, jamming its barrel into the man's chest. "Well, Lonoke," he said. "I didn't figure you in their game."

"*Their* game," gasped Lonoke. "I thought *you* were one of them. I've been trailing the bunch ever since it was cut out of our Cottonwood Bottoms herd. Every time one of the hands finds a bunch that has been cut out, it's always a day or two late, and the trail's cold. I've been trying to hook onto a hot trail all spring. I've been camping out in my sougan near our various herds, and last night I drew the high card."

Tulare got off him, still pointing the Remington his way, not yet trusting the man. "Who was it?"

"Dark," said Lonoke, getting up as far as his hunkers. "I couldn't see anything. What's your boot in this poke?"

"I told you," said Tulare. "The girl's in there."

"You had your saddle on the horse before she showed up," said Lonoke.

"Did I?" said Tulare. "You got a boot in it, too."

"I'm the Double Shank foreman," said Lonoke irritably.

"Are you?" said Tulare.

"All right, all right." Lonoke's voice was savage. "So we don't trust each other and you aren't going to tell me anything, and I'm not going to tell you. We'd better get after those cattle if we want to see where they're going."

"Take your gun out very carefully and drop it on the ground first," said Tulare.

He made Lonoke back up then and picked up the gun and stuck it in his belt. Then they worked on down the slope. They reached the cave in time to see a rider chouse the last of the steers in through the black maw of its mouth. Tulare felt something tightening inside him as he drove Lonoke ahead of him into the utter darkness. Ahead, they could hear the restless bawl of cattle booming back and forth and the incessant shuffle and thud of hoofs on the limestone.

"They'll have guards," said Lonoke.

Tulare whispered savagely: "And if we let those cows get so far ahead we can't hear them, that cooks our goose."

They groped on through the darkness, stumbling over crevices and rocks, bumping into stalagmites, knocking their heads against stalactites. Then Lonoke stopped so abruptly in front of Tulare the gun dug into his back.

"Someone's coming back!"

Tulare pulled him into a crevice, and they crouched there while the flickering light of a torch grew steadily across the undulations of limestone. Then the rider turned a corner ahead and came into full view. The torch, held above his head, cast deep shadows across the upper half of his face beneath his broad hat brim. Maybe it was the glitter of light on Lonoke's belt buckle that caught his eye, or some small movement one of them made. Either way, he was almost past them, when he turned jerkily in his saddle.

"Henry?" he said.

"All right," Tulare said, and jumped at him. The man tried to wheel his horse away, shouting, but Tulare caught his leg and pulled himself on up until he could grab the man's belt, hauling him off the horse. The buckthorn torch struck a pool of water and sizzled out, and Tulare was on the ground fighting with the man on top of him. Then the weight of another body came down on them, and Tulare grunted with the air exploding from him. He heard someone gasp, and the man he had been struggling with was suddenly a limp form across him. He got out from beneath, hearing harsh breathing beside him.

"Lonoke?"

"Yeah," said Lonoke. "He was a sucker for a rabbit punch."

"Maybe you'd like your gun back," said Tulare.

The horse had spooked and gone on down the cave, and Lonoke and Tulare removed their belts to tie the man up and stuff him in the niche they had hidden in. The cows were almost out of earshot now, and they stumbled on after them. Tulare didn't know how long it was before the bottom of the caves seemed to begin rising beneath their feet. Ahead, now and then, he caught the shine of a lantern or the flicker of torchlight. Then he began to feel the soft shuffle of loam beneath his feet instead of limestone.

"Lonoke," he said, "it looks like we're coming to another opening."

"You mean we've gone clear through the mountain?"

"That's right," said the voice from behind them. "Clear

through the mountain. And now don't try to turn around before you drop your guns."

After Tulare and Lonoke had dropped their guns, the other man lit a lantern behind them, and then walked around so they could see him. Tulare felt his mouth sag a little.

"Honest John!"

Corsica Alden thought the slap of cards would drive her crazy. The men had been playing since dark, not talking much, just sitting there at the old deal table and fluttering their cards and cutting and dealing. Corsica sat on the bunk at one side of the large room, a sullen anger pouting her lips. They had fed her some cold bacon and beans, but she was still hungry, and frightened. Maybe it was the way Henry Desha kept looking at her. He rubbed his dirty spade beard thoughtfully, studying his cards, and then his ugly, scarred head turned slightly, and his little eyes were on Corsica again.

Yawning, Sometime shoved two dollars into the pot. "Call you, Desha. Two pair."

"Pot's yours," said Desha, laying down his hand. He rose and went to the water butt, dipping out a drink. He turned toward Corsica, running one hand down his greasy *chivarras*. "Want a drink?"

"No," she said.

He hung up the dipper, moving restlessly toward her. "What do you want?"

"Never mind," said Sometime, gathering up the cards. "Let's play some more."

"The hell," said Desha. "I haven't seen a pretty girl since I was in Carlsbad. And I haven't been in Carlsbad in a month."

"This one ain't pretty."

"Wash her face and she would be."

"You aren't the one's going to wash it."

"I'll do what I please. She pleases me. Come here."

He had stepped to the bunk, trying to pull her out from where she had drawn back against the wall. She struggled violently, kicking at him, but he got a hand behind her neck and another on her arm. She twisted her head around and bit his hand. He jumped back, yelling with the pain. Then the anger twisted his face, and he jerked back his fist.

"You little. . . ."

Corsica hadn't been aware of Sometime's movement. But suddenly he was there behind Desha, grabbing that raised fist and jerking the stubby man around with it. Facing Sometime, Desha jerked free, and hauled back to slug him. Sometime kicked Desha in the stomach. Desha doubled over with a gasp, and, while he was in that position, Sometime hit him on the back of the neck. Desha sprawled, flat on the floor, and lay there trying to get his breath back with a horrible choking sound, and, when he did get it back, he began to retch.

Sometime stretched his long arms, yawned, went back to the table. "We don't touch that girl till Honest John and the others get here. I hope I've made it clear."

"Having a little trouble, Sometime?" Corsica hadn't heard the door open. It was Honest John who had spoken, but she couldn't see him. The first man in was the only one she saw. She took a small step forward, her voice breaking on the name.

"Tulare. . . ."

"Yeah," said Honest John, moving in behind Tulare. "We nabbed him in the caves."

"But they told me they found some of the twine you'd used two days ago," Corsica said. "I thought . . . I thought. . . ."

She took another faltering step toward him, and he must have seen it in her eyes, because a strange expression suddenly softened the hard line of his jaw. "You thought I was lost in there? So did Honest John. When I realized I couldn't get anywhere hunting that way, I left some of the twine rigged up to make it look like I was still in the caverns. I figured, if they thought I was lost on the inside, they wouldn't be watching for me to come in from the outside, and it would be easier to follow the cattle in."

Forty-Rod waddled in with Lonoke at the point of his stingy gun. When the Double Shank foreman saw Desha on the floor, he stopped short, surprise in the sudden tightening of his mouth.

"They got you, Henry?"

Forty-Rod chuckled. "*Got* him? Desha has been one of our brotherhood from the beginning, Lonoke."

Lonoke turned toward Forty-Rod. "But he wasn't from the Flying W."

"Do we all have to be from the Flying W?" chuckled John. "Just because Desha didn't come with Forty-Rod and me doesn't mean he isn't riding in our Murphy wagon. Desha was planted on the Double Shank two months before me and Forty-Rod moved in. When we'd bled Alden's Flying W of so many cattle that he had to declare bankruptcy, Forty-Rod and me moved over to the Double Shank."

"Our usual method of procedure," said Forty-Rod Farnum. "Several of us hire on to the outfit we have chosen for our malpractice, while the others stay on the outside. That way we have our victims approaching and departing, as it were. For this job, Sometime stayed on the outside with Peebles and several others. By the way, where is Peebles?"

"He must have been the man we met in the caves," said Tulare.

"Ah, how unfortunate for Peebles."

"It was you always rigged it so the posse wouldn't hook

onto the trail of the rustled stock till it was two or three days old?"

"One way or another," said John. "When either Desha or me got put to herding, we'd let Sometime know. If Desha and me was the only ones working the herd, that was easy. We'd just wait a day or two before reporting the steal, and by that time the trail would be cold. Sometime usually covered himself by heading for the Pecos and taking the cattle north in the water for several miles so the trail never did lead directly to Walnut Cañon. Even if someone did find cattle sign in the cañon, they'd think the cows had been driven on through and headed toward the border."

Tulare was glancing at Corsica now, something intent in his eyes. She was trying to understand when Lonoke spoke.

"But why hold the rustled stock here?"

Chuckling, Forty-Rod Farnum waved a hand at the dark man who had come in with them. "This is Marquette Duval. He has been acting as trustee for the court of bankruptcy in Eddy County these last few years. The duties of a trustee include collecting and reducing to cash the property of bankrupt estates. Said property includes cattle, naturally. Take Edward Alden's Flying W last year, for instance. After we had finished bleeding Alden's spread, there were only three hundred steers left. When Alden went into bankruptcy, Duval, under the direction of the courts, rounded up the three hundred steers and shipped them. At the same time, we took the fifteen hundred steers we'd been holding here and shipped them."

"I had made arrangements to sell that many beforehand," said Duval, "so when the eighteen hundred Flying W steers arrived in Kansas City, the packers accepted them as all having been sent by the court."

Corsica was beginning to sense it now, what Tulare was

200

trying to tell her. If Forty-Rod and Honest John were revealing all this, it could only mean one thing. Then what did Tulare want? He was still staring at her as Forty-Rod began shuffling back and forth in front of the bunk, hunting for something.

"As trustee," said Forty-Rod, "Duval's signature on any check or bank draft connected with the estate makes it perfectly valid. Thus, when the packing company paid him for the eighteen hundred Flying W cattle with a check drawn on an Eastern bank, he deposited the check in that bank. Then he withdrew enough to cover the fifteen hundred steers we shipped from Hobbs, and we got our split. That left the amount to cover the court's three hundred steers still in the Eastern bank. By check, Duval switched that last amount to the Carlsbad bank, where it would be whenever the court wanted it. Thus he has the amount they were expecting deposited where they expected it to be deposited, and the check stubs to make all his books tally."

"Naturally the courts never see the stub for the original eighteen hundred steers," said Duval, smiling without much mirth. "Only for their three hundred. But as they never knew anything about the other fifteen hundred anyway, and all my books are in order, why should they question?"

"And we ain't never had to touch the brand," said Honest John. "The come-down of nine out of ten wet cattle operators these last years has been the hide inspectors at the shipping points. For every one rustler that gets a bunch of decorated cattle through, nine others are caught by the inspector when he spots those blotted brands. But we ship under the same marks the cattle wore all the time, and thumb our noses at the inspectors."

Forty-Rod had found what he wanted. With much grunting and puffing, he squatted down and hauled a jug from beneath the bunk. Corsica was hardly aware of that. Tulare had finally gotten it across to her. His eyes kept going from hers to the lantern on the table, and she understood. It was the only light in the room, and Forty-Rod and John were about finished, and there wasn't much time left.

"Maybe the courts don't question you because you have everything in order when they want it," said Sometime. "We do. It wasn't eighteen hundred Flying W steers. It was two thousand. I told you, Duval. Did you bring our split for that other two hundred?"

Duval's smile faded, and he held out one hand. "I told you, Sometime, you were mistaken. . . ."

"Sometime wasn't mistaken," said Forty-Rod, and put the big jug under one arm so he could get the Krider Derringer out from beneath his dirty red vest. "We have procrastinated about this too long. I think it had better be settled up now. You won't get out of Lost Valley unless you cough up, Duval."

Corsica saw that Tulare had a chunk of lead in his hand, and he was speaking to Forty-Rod. "What caliber does that stingy gun throw, Forty-Rod?"

They all turned to Tulare, and Corsica wondered if he wasn't doing it to give her that chance. She was almost near enough now. Forty-Rod looked at the mashed bullet in Tulare's hand.

"Isn't that rather irrelevant?" he said.

"They couldn't find the bullet Edward Alden was supposed to have shot himself with," said Tulare. "They found him at his desk with one bullet out of his own gun and his head blown apart, but they couldn't find the bullet. I located this embedded in the wall of the living room. I figure he was shot there and dragged to his desk. . . ."

"You're the one!" said Lonoke.

"Is that why you tried to block me when I first came?" said Tulare.

"I thought maybe you were some kind of investigator," said Lonoke. "I was sick of lawmen. The sheriff had been around off and on for six months, getting in my way and messing things up and spooking our cattle, and he never did anything about the rustlers. Pierce hired a couple of stock dicks that only caused us a mountain heap of trouble."

"You missed that one," Sometime told Duval.

"Not entirely," said Duval. "After our little talk the other day, I did some enquiring. The court must have brought in Tulare without my knowledge. In the records, I found an order signed by Judge Faber authorizing a marshal to inspect the premises of the late Edward Alden before they were turned into the hands of the receivers. That must have been eight months back. Have you been working on the case ever since, Marshal Tulare?"

"Deputy marshal," said Tulare. "All the other county and private officers had worked in the open without any success, so when the federal government stepped in, they didn't want their man known. That's why they appeared to refuse Alden's request for a marshal. The marshal in this district was too well-known for any undercover work, so he deputized me. I'd been doing this kind of work off and on for the federals. I had to get an order from the courts to search Alden's premises, since the estate was in their hands."

Again Tulare had let his eyes stray to Corsica while he was talking, and she realized this was it, and, when he suddenly tossed the chunk of lead at Forty-Rod, saying—"See if this fits your stingy gun."—Corsica seized the moment Tulare had given her, while all their attention was on him, and swept one arm out and knocked the lantern off the table. It crashed to the floor; there was a last flare of light, then utter darkness.

For a moment, she couldn't recognize anything clearly in the bedlam of shouts and scuffling feet and shifting bodies. Then one voice raised above the others.

"Get that Tulare, get that Tulare. . . ."

The shots rocked the room, and someone else shouted. "Stop shooting, you'll hit one of us!"

"Never mind!" yelled another man, and it sounded like Sometime. "I got him. I got Tulare."

VII

They had quit shuffling around, and someone was rummaging around for the lantern. The man struck a match along the leg of his Levi's with a hissing sound, and adjusted the wick on the lantern till the flame rose to shine through the broken glass. Standing above the one he had shot, Sometime got a brief glimpse of the men in the room. Forty-Rod stood over by the door with Duval, and Honest John was bringing the lantern over to throw light across the body at Sometime's feet.

"You damn' fool," he said. "You shot Desha!"

None of them needed to speak. Forty-Rod was through the door first, and then Duval, and Honest John snuffed out the lantern so they wouldn't make a target. Sometime found his over-and-under gun leaning in a corner and stumbled over Desha's body on his way out. False dawn lit the sky, and he could see the valley dimly, spreading away beneath the slope upon which stood the shack, the herd of cattle shifting beneath a haze of their own dust in the bottoms. The caverns themselves were formed by seepage of water and erosion, and the men had diverted one of the underground springs in the cave to form a small stream that ran through the middle of the basin for the cattle. The rugged mesas and ridges of the bad-lands surrounded the valley completely, their harsh top lands silhouetted against the pink sky.

"Spread out!" called Forty-Rod from ahead. "Don't let them reach the caves."

"Now, Forty-Rod," Honest John told him, "you know they'll git lost if they ever reach the caves."

"Listen, you sentimental old fool," shouted Forty-Rod, "if you come across Tulare and don't let daylight through him, I'll put so many corrugations in your esophagus with this stingy gun you'll sound like a turkey gobbler when you take a drink!"

"But he saved my life. Not only once. He saved it twice. I. . . ."

"I don't care how many times he saved your life. I told you he'd just cause us trouble. Every time you take a hankering to somebody, we wind up like this. . . ."

Then they were out of earshot, and Sometime was working through the rocks toward the upper slopes above the level of the shack so he would have a wider scope. Sometime knew, without having to see them, that Honest John was working the mid-slopes, and Forty-Rod the bottomlands. They had been together so long their teamwork had become a tacit, unspoken thing. Sometime began to slow down now, settling into his languid, unhurried movements, slipping from rock to rock without any wasted motion. He squatted down behind a cholla to scan the stretch of mesquite ahead, and started to yawn. It made him realize he hadn't slept all night. He shrugged. Finish this and he could sleep as long as he liked. And he would finish it. None of them had a gun, Tulare or Corsica or Lonoke. He felt no particular qualms about shooting them unarmed. If it fell to him, he would do it, that's all.

Then he caught the first movement ahead of him and stopped a while. It wasn't repeated. Waiting? He pulled his lever, and that would be the .30-30 load in the top barrel. Then he was jerking toward the rattling sound on the slope below him, and, just as he saw the rock bouncing across the shale there, he heard the man yell from behind him. It was Danny Lonoke who had thrown the stone from the rimrock above to attract Sometime's attention. He made a big screaming, yelling, hurtling blot in Sometime's sight, and Sometime squeezed his trigger and the gun jumped in his hand with a roar, and then Lonoke's body struck him, and he went over backward with all the air exploding from his body. His head struck the talus with a force that seemed to detonate his brain, and that was all.

Forty-Rod Farnum didn't understand it at first, when he came across the maguey. He squatted there, holding that jug in one hand, his gun hardly perceptible in his other great hammy fist. Some of the maguey's tough, stringy branches had been freshly stripped off. He took a pull at the jug, trying to understand that. Maguey branches? Stripped off. He took another swig. Then he shook the jug, holding it up to his ear. A sad expression crossed his bleary eyes. Reluctantly he set it down. Henry Desha must have imbibed before he got hold of it. Curse Henry Desha. Or was it profane to vilify the dead? He took a last look at the maguey, and hoisted his ponderous bulk onward, moving through the mesquite of the lower slopes in a crouch, breathing heavily with the effort.

The shot from above startled him, and he turned that way, pulling his gun up. *John?* He almost called the name. Then he began to climb upward, tremendous thighs threatening to burst his jeans with every surging step, sweat leaking down the creases in his fat face. They hadn't been making for the caves, then; they had been trying to get out through the bad-lands. Clever, in a way. Foolish, in another. He had to stop and rest more than once. The last time he stopped wasn't to rest. He crouched there, staring at the body sprawled across the talus from above him. He waited a long time before he moved on up and knelt beside Sometime.

Sometime had fallen or been knocked backward, striking his head on a large boulder. His over-and-under gun was gone. Forty-Rod knew a sudden anger. It hadn't been anger before this; he had felt no particular rancor toward Tulare or Lonoke or the girl; it had just been something to do. Now he knew an anger. He had worked with Sometime a long while. He had liked Sometime, almost as much as Honest John. The laziest man in New Mexico, probably, but he had liked him.

Forty-Rod's eyes were small and mean as he turned to read the sign in directions away from Sometime. There was a flushed look to his face that hadn't come from the hard climb. He turned to scan the valley below him. Nothing. He moved toward the rimrock farther up. Then he reached the second maguey. It had been stripped of its branches the same as the other one. An idea began to form in Forty-Rod's mind. He re-membered Honest John's telling him how good Tulare had been with a rope, and this is what prompted the idea to form in his mind. But why should they need it, if they had Some-time's over-and-under?

He stopped moving suddenly, to the scratching sound above him. The slope broke into a series of narrow benches here, reaching on up to the rimrock itself. Some of the benches screened any mesquite and maguey and cactus. Forty-Rod's eyes grew smaller as the sound came again, and his fat lips pulled in tight.

"Tulare?" he called. There was no answer, and Forty-Rod began to move upward, the anger in him all mixed up in the mild alcoholic haze that had enveloped him for most of his life. "I'm coming, Tulare. You liquidated Sometime. That was your last malapropism. You won't get a chance to make any more mistakes. I'm going to triturate your cerebrum the same way I did Alden's. You wondered if that chunk of lead fitted my stingy gun? Perfectly, Tulare, perfectly." He was puffing now, hauling his enormous belly over the first ledge, his sweating face turned upward, waiting for the muzzle of Sometime's over-and-under to poke across one of the benches above. They would have to do it that way, even if they were screened from him by the bushes. They would have to show the gun to shoot, and that would be their mistake. "Alden got too inquisitive, Tulare, like yourself. He got suspicious of Duval for some reason, and instigated a motion at the meeting of his creditors to investigate Duval's records." He had to abandon the ledge and began to work up the next steep stretch of rock-covered cliff. His hand was bleeding now, and his blood was pounding in his ears, and he didn't mean to stop till he got them. "And now you'll get your cranium sparged just like Alden did. I'm coming, Tulare, and you. . . ."

It wasn't what he had expected, and perhaps that was what affected his reaction. For that one astonishing moment, he stared upward at the thing hissing down at him from above, and then, even as he jerked aside, he knew what they had been doing with that maguey. He had moved too late, and he didn't try to get away after that. Without struggling against the agony of constriction, he stared upward, eyes popping out, and in that last moment saw them lurching forward up there, pulled out from against the cliff by his tremendous weight, and he fired.

Honest John didn't want to do this. Honest John had liked

the boy, and he didn't want to do it. He could have done it, when he had first found Tulare in the caves, of course. He should have. He should have left Tulare down in that pit. But, somehow, it hadn't been in him. And now this. He guessed Forty-Rod was right; he was just an old sentimentalist. That didn't pay in this game. It had always caused trouble before.

John moved reluctantly through the mesquite, trying not to rattle it. Not as spry as he used to be. Ten years ago he could have tracked this brush with no more noise than a sidewinder slipping through the sand. He was moving up toward the rimrock where the shot had come from. He hoped it meant the job had been done. He hoped he would meet Forty-Rod, and Forty-Rod would tell him. . . .

He stopped then, crouching in the fringe of mesquite, because he had met Forty-Rod. The fat man lay on his back with his face contorted into a horrible mask, the swollen tongue thrust between the lips, the bloodshot eyes popped out like a frog's. John moved over to the man, forcing himself to make some kind of an examination. There were no bullet wounds. He didn't want to accept the other answer. He looked up at the rising wall of rimrock, cut into gigantic steps by a series of benches, and he wondered if Forty-Rod had fallen far. He spotted the fat man's gun a few feet away, and then it began to grow in him. It should have been anger, really, because he and Forty-Rod had been together a long time. But it wasn't anger, somehow. It was more a realization. Tulare had been unarmed, and Forty-Rod had carried iron. In the ten years he had known the fat man, John had never seen an armed man stop Forty-Rod. And Tulare had been unarmed. And here was Forty-Rod.

Moving down the more open shale, he saw them finally. They had reached the mouth of the cave and were halting there. He tried to reach them before they spotted him, but he was still out of range when he saw them move back into the maw of the cavern, the girl disappearing first, then Tulare stopping for a last moment as if to look backward. When John reached it, they had already melted into the blackness. He slipped off his boots and began to work his way in. Soon there was nothing but that eternal, pitch-black midnight all about him.

"You're a fool if you think you can find your way through here in the dark, boy," he said. There was no answer, and he stopped to listen a moment. He heard someone breathing. He moved toward the sound cautiously. "Damn you, boy," he began again in that querulous tone, "this is the hardest cinch I ever pulled. I should be right cut up with you for digging Forty-Rod's grave, but somehow I still don't want to do this. Why did you have to follow us in like that? If you'd stayed out there and busted your bronc's, we could've been friends. I liked you, boy."

"I had a job, John, and. . . ."

The thunder of Honest John's brass-framed Prescott drowned Tulare's voice. With the gun hot in his hand John stood till the echoes had died, waiting.

"If you wanted to get me talking. . . ."

Again the gun drowned out Tulare's voice, bucking in John's hand. With the echoes hiding the sound of his feet, John ran forward a few paces, then stopped again as they died. Tulare's voice came again.

"I said if you wanted to get me talking so you could shoot at the sound of my voice, you better try something else. These caves twist the sound all around till you can't tell where it's coming from."

John held his fire this time, realizing Tulare was right. He began to slide forward. He kicked some loose shale and drew back suddenly. The shale had clattered a moment, across bare rock, and then had ceased making any sound at all. With one foot, John felt across the limestone floor, stiffening as his toe reached the edge of the rock. He was standing on one of the ledges that formed the trail, one side dropping off into an unplumbed pit.

He wiped the back of his free hand across his forehead, and it came away clammy with sweat. He curled his finger around the spur trigger of his Prescott, and slid down the wall, trying to listen again.

"I don't want to do this, boy." He stopped, thinking he heard someone breathing. "Why didn't you stay out and bust your bronc's?" He lifted the gun a little, then lowered it, remembering Forty-Rod. "I don't want to do this." He crept on forward, trying to hold his own breath. "I should be riled at you for what you did to Forty-Rod, but I'm not, dammit." He shifted hands with his gun to wipe the sweat off his right palm, then shifted back again.

It was the sound then, and the movement so close to him it brought his gun up with a startled jerk, and he pulled on the trigger. The cave was filled with a roaring thunder. Maybe he sensed it coming out of the blackness, or maybe he had already felt it. He jerked backward, emptying his gun into the cavern, but he hadn't jumped soon enough or far enough. It caught him under one upflung arm and around the neck, and jerked tightly.

"Tulare?" he shouted crazily, because it was something he didn't understand in that instant, and then he did understand it, and he should have known from the beginning, after seeing Forty-Rod. He was jerking wildly to get away, and suddenly there was nothing solid beneath him. He felt it jerk once more on him, and then he was through feeling anything but the mournful sigh of his own falling.

★ ★ ★ ★ ★

Tulare crouched there a moment after John's last shout, panting. The girl was between him and the wall, and her body was a vibrant warmth against his.

"What happened?" she said.

"I don't know." He spoke hoarsely. "I'm going to see. You stay here."

"No, Bob. . . ."

"You want to keep running away?" he said. "We can't go back any farther without getting lost. This is the last horse to ride, Corsica. You stay here no matter what happens, but I've got to tell you before I go. When I came here, I was a deputy marshal, and I was supposed to be after the rustled cattle and the men who rustled them. But I wasn't after the cows. Or the rustlers. Maybe I wasn't doing my job. I don't know. All I know is I wasn't coming after them. Ever since you disappeared in here with Sometime, I was only thinking about one thing, and I didn't come in after the cows or the rustlers. . . ."

"I know, I know!" There was something fierce in her voice.

"That's all I care about, then," he said, and heard her take a breath, and he knew it was to say his name, but she didn't, because he was already crawling away. He felt his way across the limestone, moving with as little sound as possible. He brought up against a wall, bumping his head. Then the call came from somewhere ahead.

"John?"

It sounded like Lonoke, and Tulare took the chance. "Watch it, Lonoke."

"Tulare?" said Lonoke, and Tulare could hear him moving nearer. "I thought I saw Honest John come in here."

"You did," said Tulare. "Watch it."

He crouched there while Lonoke moved stealthily toward

him. He could hear the scrape of the man's boots, his breathing. Then Lonoke bumped into him, jumped back. Tulare was on his feet with the click of Lonoke's lever in his ears.

"It's Tulare," he said.

"Then where's John?" Lonoke was silent a moment. "I'll light this lantern."

There was a tiny sound, the flare of a match. The reddish light fell across the limestone floor first, showing them to be on a ledge. Tulare moved over to the lip, staring off into the pit, and he heard the girl make a small, choked sound behind him and realized she understood, too.

"I found Forty-Rod out near the rimrock," said Lonoke. "Looked like he'd been strangled to death."

"I made a rope out of maguey," said Tulare. "The Mexicans cure it in the sun and soak it in water to make it supple, but I didn't have time for that."

There was something incredulous in Lonoke's voice. "You mean . . . you got Forty-Rod that way . . . ?"

"John, too," said Tulare. "I used the flash of his gun to throw at. Must have hooked him. He started struggling. The rope pulled out of my hands. I see why, now."

Lonoke shoved a small rock off the edge with his foot. They listened for it to strike bottom, and heard nothing. The three of them looked at one another. Finally the girl forced herself to speak.

"Then there's only Duval."

Lonoke patted the over-and-under gun. "Duval's sitting out on the rimrock with a load of buckshot in his leg. I figure he can lead us back out through these caves. He said they blazed the trail with axes on the walls."

He held the lantern up to lead the way toward the mouth, and Tulare got on the right side of Corsica so he could take

213

her arm. "We'll get a crew in here to drive those Double Shank cows out. I guess that about finishes my job. Yours, too, Corsica. What are you going to do now?"

"I don't know exactly."

"Don't you?"

The lantern cast her face into a soft light, turning upward toward him, and it was the way she said his name. "Bob. . . ."

"Your Flying W hasn't been disposed of yet by the court," he said. "It would take a little money to get it out of the hands of the receivers, but I haven't spent all my government checks for fancy saddles. Do you think a one-armed ex-marshal could run a spread that size . . . if he had the help of a girl who already knew the outfit?"

"I know he could," she said.

"Then I know he *will*," he said.

THE SHADOW IN RENEGADE BASIN

LES SAVAGE, JR.

The novels and stories of Les Savage, Jr., have always been famous for their excitement, style, and historical accuracy. But this accuracy frequently ran afoul of editors in the 1950s. Only now is Savage's work finally being restored and presented in all its original glory. Finally, the realism, the humanity, and the honesty of his classic tales are allowed to shine through. This volume collects three of Savage's greatest tales, including the title novella, a brilliant account of a cursed basin where the mineral deposits look like blood, and where treachery has wiped out all the residents . . . except one.

___ 4896-5 $4.50 US/$5.50 CAN

MAX BRAND

MEN BEYOND THE LAW

These three short novels showcase Max Brand doing what he does best: exploring the wild, often dangerous life beyond the constraints of cities, beyond the reach of civilization . . . beyond the law. Whether he's a desperate man fleeing the tragic results of a gunfight, an innocent young man who stumbles onto the loot from a bank robbery, or the gentle giant named Bull Hunter—one of Brand's most famous characters—each protagonist is out on his own, facing two unknown frontiers: the Wild West . .. and his own future.

___4873-6 $4.50 US/$5.50 CAN

SAFETY McTEE

Here, in paperback for the first time, restored from his own typescripts, are three prime examples of Max Brand at his rousing best. In "Little Sammy Green," a son has a difficult time living up to the reputation of his gunfighter father, until fate forces him to prove himself. "Black Sheep" is the extraordinary story of a nine-year-old tomboy who comes up with a scheme to win an outlaw his freedom, even though it puts her own life in jeopardy. And "Safety McTee" tells of a gunfighter who earned his nickname by merely wounding, not killing, his opponents. But when he's forced to shoot an old man in self-defense, he finds himself hunted by a lynch mob that doesn't appreciate his past mercies.

___4528-1 $4.50 US/$5.50 CAN

Dorchester Publishing Co., Inc.
P.O. Box 6640
Wayne, PA 19087-8640

Please add $1.75 for shipping and handling for the first book and $.50 for each book thereafter. NY, NYC, and PA residents, please add appropriate sales tax. No cash, stamps, or C.O.D.s. All orders shipped within 6 weeks via postal service book rate. Canadian orders require $2.00 extra postage and must be paid in U.S. dollars through a U.S. banking facility.

Name_____
Address_____
City_____State_____Zip_____
I have enclosed $_____ in payment for the checked book(s).
Payment <u>must</u> accompany all orders. ❏ Please send a free catalog.
CHECK OUT OUR WEBSITE! www.dorchesterpub.com

MAX BRAND

THE LEGEND OF THUNDER MOON

Thunder Moon was born white. But as a boy he was captured by a mighty Cheyenne brave who needed a son, and was raised in the ways of his father's tribe. As Thunder Moon grew, he learned Cheyenne culture and sought honor through warfare and hunting to overcome the stigma of his light skin. Yet there are some traditions Thunder Moon cannot accept. One of these is the self-torture of the Sun Dance, the major rite of passage to adulthood for braves. He has to find another way to prove himself worthy in the eyes of his adopted people. His chance comes in a test so daring, so courageous, that no man can doubt his manhood. Thunder Moon will lead a raid against the Cheyenne's fiercest enemies, the scourge of the Plains—the Comanches!

___4583-4 $4.50 US/$5.50 CAN

Dorchester Publishing Co., Inc.
P.O. Box 6640
Wayne, PA 19087-8640

Please add $1.75 for shipping and handling for the first book and $.50 for each book thereafter. NY, NYC, and PA residents, please add appropriate sales tax. No cash, stamps, or C.O.D.s. All orders shipped within 6 weeks via postal service book rate. Canadian orders require $2.00 extra postage and must be paid in U.S. dollars through a U.S. banking facility.

Name_____
Address_____
City_____State_____Zip_____
I have enclosed $_____ in payment for the checked book(s).
Payment <u>must</u> accompany all orders. ❑ Please send a free catalog.
CHECK OUT OUR WEBSITE! www.dorchesterpub.com

MAX BRAND

SLUMBER MOUNTAIN

Here, for the first time in paperback, are three of Max Brand's best short novels, all restored to their original glory from Brand's own typescripts and presented just as he intended. "Outland Crew" is an exciting tale of gold fever and survival in a frontier mining town. In "The Coward," a man humiliated in a gunfight finds a fiendishly clever way of exacting revenge. And in "Slumber Mountain," Brand presents a harrowing story of man versus the wilderness as a trapper fights for his life against the mighty wolf known as Silver King.

___4442-0 $4.99 US/$5.99 CAN

Collected here for the first time in paperback are three of Max Brand's greatest short novels, all restored to their original splendor, just as the author intended. In "The Red Bandanna," Clancy Morgan returns to town to warn his best friend, Danny Travis, that Bill Orping is heading there, looking for a confrontation. But when he gets there he finds that Orping has arrived before him and was shot in the back—and it looks like Danny was the killer. "His Name His Fortune" is the story of a young gambler who falls in love with the daughter of a wealthy rancher who despises him. And in the final short novel, "Soft Metal," Larry Givain, fleeing from a posse, meets a beautiful woman at a deserted cabin belonging to one of the men in the posse. Her brother is also holed up in the cabin, pursed by a notorious gunfighter. With death drawing ever nearer, Givain realizes his life will never be the same again.

___4698-9 $4.50 US/$5.50 CAN

Dorchester Publishing Co., Inc.
P.O. Box 6640
Wayne, PA 19087-8640

Please add $1.75 for shipping and handling for the first book and $.50 for each book thereafter. NY, NYC, and PA residents, please add appropriate sales tax. No cash, stamps, or C.O.D.s. All orders shipped within 6 weeks via postal service book rate. Canadian orders require $2.00 extra postage and must be paid in U.S. dollars through a U.S. banking facility.

Name_____
Address_____
City_____ State_____ Zip_____
I have enclosed $_____ in payment for the checked book(s).
Payment <u>must</u> accompany all orders. ❑ Please send a free catalog.

ALAN LeMAY
SPANISH CROSSING

The stories in this classic collection, in paperback for the first time, include "The Wolf Hunter," a gripping tale of a loner who makes his living hunting wolves for bounty and the crafty coyote who torments him. Old Man Coffee, one of LeMay's most memorable characters, finds himself in the midst of a murder mystery in "The Biscuit Shooter." In "Delayed Action," Old Man Coffee's challenge is to vindicate a lawman who's been falsely accused. These and many other fine stories display the talent and skill of one of the West's greatest storytellers.

THE
SMOKY
YEARS
Alan LeMay

The cattle barons. They were tough, weathered men like Dusty King and Lew Gordon, who had sweated and worked along the great cattle trails to form a partnership whose brand was burned on herds beyond measure. they had fought hard for what they had. . . and they would fight even harder to keep it. And they know a fight is coming. It is as thick in the wind as trail dust. Newcomers like Ben Thorpe are moving in, desperate to get their hands on the miles and miles of grazing land— land that King and Gordon want, and that Thorpe needs to survive. No one knows how the war will end, but one thing is certain—only one empire can survive.

LAURAN PAINE

THE KILLER GUN

It is no ordinary gun. It is specially designed to help its owner kill a man. George Mars has customized a Colt revolver so it will fire when it is on half cock, saving the time it takes to pull back the hammer before firing. But then the gun is stolen from Mars's shop. Mars has engraved his name on it but, as the weapon passes from hand to hand, owner to owner, killer to killer, his identity becomes as much of a mystery as why possession of the gun skews the odds in any duel. And the legend of the killer gun grows with each newly slain man.

___4875-2 $4.50 US/$5.50 CAN

Dorchester Publishing Co., Inc.
P.O. Box 6640
Wayne, PA 19087-8640